fax me a
bagel

sharon kahn

BERKLEY PRIME CRIME, NEW YORK

FAX ME A BAGEL

A Berkley Prime Crime Book / published by arrangement with Scribner, a division of Simon & Schuster, Inc.

PRINTING HISTORY
Scribner hardcover edition / 1998
Berkley Prime Crime mass-market edition / July 2001

ISBN: 0-425-18046-8

Berkley Prime Crime Books are published
by The Berkley Publishing Group,
a division of Penguin Putnam Inc.,
375 Hudson Street, New York, New York 10014.
The name BERKLEY PRIME CRIME and the BERKLEY PRIME CRIME
design are trademarks belonging to Penguin Putnam Inc.

PRINTED IN THE UNITED STATES OF AMERICA

10 9 8 7 6 5 4 3 2 1

In loving memory of my parents,
MORRIS KAHN AND GLADYS KAHN GILMAN,
*who believed in me and taught me to see things
as they really are.*

acknowledgments

To my family—always in my heart: David, Suzy, Jon and Nancy, Emma and Camille.

To Lindsy Van Gelder, who first heard my voice; Nancy Bell, who showed me where to use it; and Ruthe Winegarten, whose wit and wisdom were always there for me. Thanks to those special people who offered support, advice, and encouragement during the writing of this book: Suzanne Bloomfield—dear friend and life booster; The Shoal Creek Writers: Dena Garcia, Eileen Joyce, Karen Casey Fitzjerrell, and Julie Rennecker; and to Pamela Brandt and Nancy L. Hendrickson. Thanks to Trillium, too.

The Bagel Bible, Second Edition, by Marilyn Bagel, Globe Pequot Press, 1995, provided fascinating background and has been the basis for many press accounts of bagel lore.

To my extraordinary agent, Helen Rees, who trusted me and waited, and to the mystery writer's dream editor, Susanne Kirk, executive editor of Scribner, I am most grateful. My appreciation also to Joan Mazmanian of the Helen Rees Agency, to Elizabeth Barden of Scribner, and Estelle Laurence, for guiding the book through its paces with such care.

I salute those in congregational life whose values transcend all adversity.

Finally, I hold dear the memory of Perrin Lowrey of the Vassar College English Department, who first told me I could do it.

chapter
1
....

You haven't lived until you've died in Eternal, Texas.

This particular death hit me on a personal level—I saw it happen. The shock doesn't wear off even by bedtime, when I drag myself to my computer and type a quick e-mail message to my friend Nan in Seattle. It's midnight in Texas, ten o'clock on the West Coast, and I know Nan will be hovering near her screen. We've saved a fortune on phone calls since we discovered electronic mail.

No salutation—we never bother:

E-mail from: Ruby
To: Nan
Subject: *Oy*

Today a woman dropped dead in the bagel bakery right in front of my eyes. More later.

Nan's used to cryptic messages from me when I'm in a hurry, but I know this one will have her reeling.

The Day from Hell starts at midmorning—one of those August in Texas "ninety-nine and ninety-niners"— ninety-nine degree temperature and ninety-nine percent humidity. I feel bagel lust coming on, so I throw on my day-off uniform, a pair of cutoffs with a split in the thigh I don't notice until I'm halfway to the bagel bakery. On top I'm wearing the *Born to Bake* tee shirt Joshie gave me last year as a reminder of his culinarily deprived childhood at the hands of a mother who collected gorgeous cookbooks just to look at the food. It's barely eleven o'clock, so I figure, dress-wise, I'm safe from congregational eyes—after all, who eats lunch at eleven?

Wrong. The place is a zoo. I have to stand in line and take a number from the machine, which turns out to be number 46—my age. Not a good omen. Even though they're up to number 36, I know I ought to turn tail while I have the chance, but what can I tell you—the thought of a piping hot bagel washed down by a freezing can of Diet Coke seduces me.

I'm standing in line daydreaming like I usually do in crowds, not noticing anyone around me, when someone taps my shoulder from behind. I turn around and look. It's Essie Sue Margolis, aka Honorary Permanent Vice-Chairman of the temple board, dressed in a white silk suit untouched by human hands. I plotz. When Stu was alive he called her the Terminator in Drag. Stu, so shy and soft-spoken in public, survived rabbinic life by privately zeroing in on any sign of phoniness. He had Essie Sue down pat.

She looks at the slightly pinkish spot on my *Born to Bake* shirt where the pizza sauce wouldn't wash out, offhandedly dusts off her creased white silks in case anything from me got on her, and then gazes at me with a sad smile that would melt chicken schmaltz.

"Ruby Rothman, how *are* you?" she says. Essie Sue has been giving me her condolence smile for a year and a half now. A full year after Stu was killed, I repeated an innocuous joke in her presence and she told me she thought humor was highly inappropriate so soon after.

Essie Sue's mission when she first laid eyes on me twenty-one years ago was to see that I was never "inappropriate." She landed on our doorstep the day we moved to town. At the time, I was taking doggie-do out of the baby's hands and wondering if the water in the new house had been turned on. Essie Sue was undaunted by mere plumbing—this was a woman who would dress to take the garbage out, if she were ever in such an unfortunate position.

That's the short version of who Essie Sue Margolis is. Even though I'm not in her power anymore, whenever I run into her the first thing I think of is—what's she going to try to make me do? One of the first things Essie Sue wanted to change about me was my "unruly" dark red hair—not a chance, of course. I like it short and curly—it's easy to care for. She said Jews weren't supposed to have green eyes and red hair and didn't I think red hair, even dark red hair, wasn't dignified? For what it was worth, I told her lots of biblical figures were redheads. Some were, actually, but this was not a woman who sweated the details. She also didn't understand why I became a computer consultant in addition to my true calling as Official Wife, but since the job was freelance, she chose to ignore it.

Essie Sue's totally nondescript sister Marla is standing in line beside her, holding on to their number 47. Marla was number 2 in their childhood hierarchy and still is. She and her daughter Glenda moved here, when Glenda was a child, to be near Essie Sue and her husband. Marla looks like Essie Sue with the air let out. They're tall, and both sport shades of blond—Essie Sue's short, sculpted cut has been Golden Honey for years now, so Marla is stuck with the Ash Wednesday pageboy—three shades lighter but still coordinated. Essie Sue goes with her to buy all her clothes, I hear, and they apparently compare notes to make sure they never wear clashing colors. Guess who does the coordinating?

Essie Sue has now pushed Marla in front of her, and I'm hoping it'll cut down on the conversation. It's strange to find Marla standing in front of Essie Sue for any reason—it's usually the other way around. I know why, though—Essie Sue has put Marla in front so Marla can be the one to give the bagel order to my friend Milt Aboud, the Lebanese version of the Pillsbury doughboy and owner of The Hot Bagel. Essie Sue hasn't spoken to Milt for twenty years, but she's not about to let a lifetime grudge make her miss out on the best bakery in Eternal. Marla gets along with Milt these days, and besides, she doesn't have the energy for grudges.

*   *   *

I'm finally inching up to the head of the line. Milt calls my number 46. Just as I'm ready to give my usual order, Essie Sue says, "Ruby, darling, you know my hubby's blood sugar problem. He has to eat lunch on the stroke of twelve so you won't mind if Marla and I get in front of you."

No question mark here. Essie Sue doesn't know from question marks—declarative is her permanent mode. She says it and expects you to get it. She steps in front of me, exchanges our numbers, and pushes Marla right to the counter. Marla hands Milt the number and gives Essie Sue's order, plus a dozen cinnamon raisin (it figures) for herself, with a special almond raisin on top for the extra. Essie Sue turns her back to Milt and concentrates on me.

"So what brings you here so early in the day?" she says.

"Just indulging in my midweek bagel craving," I say, trying to anticipate her next move, which I assume will be some not-so-subtle reference to my expanding waistline. I attempt an end run.

"Nice that they give the thirteenth bagel for free, isn't it?" I say.

"Baker's dozen," she says. "They all have to do that."

Of course, Milt is the only one in town who does, but that doesn't stop her.

"I only eat the thirteenth bagel, myself," she says.

"Excuse me?"

"That's the only one I eat," she says, looking at me as if I'm too impaired to understand the obvious. "I allow myself one garlic bagel a week, and I give the rest to Hal—he can use the extra calories. He likes a poppyseed on Mondays and Thursdays, plain on Saturday and Sunday, and onion on Tuesday, Wednesday, and Friday. Pumpernickel I save for people who drop in."

I stare at her in silent wonder, not dreaming of asking how come. This I learned years ago—mine not to question why. Another conversation stopper, I tell myself. I mean, what do you actually *say* to this? Realizing that Milt had more luck than brains to escape from years of conversation with this woman, I simply nod my head mindlessly and hope that my turn comes soon.

Milt's new place is cavernous, so the air conditioning's lukewarm and has to compete with hot ovens from the back of the counter. His bakers and helpers are in full view—filling orders at long wooden tables facing the eating area. This morning they look like droopy storks with their grungy white hats wilting in that midday heat.

I'm getting very thirsty when I finally hear my new number called.

"Your turn, Ruby—don't wait all day." Milt reaches out and turns my shoulder back toward the counter. We exchange a look, but say nothing about our common enemy, who, having made her purchase, is holding her sister's arm as she snakes them both around the tables of seated customers to see if there's anyone in the room worth hello-ing.

"You should talk," I say. "I feel as though I've been in line forever. Now that this place is the gold mine I predicted it would be, how about some more air conditioners? You can afford it."

"Wish we could talk," Milt says as he fills my usual order for twelve plain to take home and an almond raisin as a treat for now, "but this line of customers would stone me. This ain't a good day." He wipes his neck with his big white sleeve and reties his apron around his doughboy stomach.

"Come on, Milt—you just don't want to let me in on the millions you're racking up in this place."

"Millions from bagels? Try it sometime."

He changes the subject to the usual. "When are you going to help me shop for my fax machine, Ruby? What good does it do me to have a techie in my life if I don't get any benefit from it? The business customers love to fax lunch orders—it's the new toy." Milt reaches back to get my overstuffed bagel bag, which has been filled in about two seconds. "I won't charge you if you'll set a date."

"No, go ahead and charge me," I say. "I can't do it this week. Definitely next. I thought you couldn't talk now."

"Now who's doing the avoiding, Ruby?"

"Soon. I promise, Milt. And just for your information, faxes aren't new—you're probably the last business in town without one."

He makes a last try before going to the next customer. "They're toys and you know it."

Now for the worst part—I have to get out of here without running into yet *more* yentas. Hello-ing is definitely not my cup of tea, and besides, I hate spending an extra half hour just working my way to the front door. I've learned that being a rabbi's wife is not something you graduate from in this life. I once thought that maybe with Stu gone—much as I miss him—my title would go, too. No such luck.

Of course, my role would have been easier if I'd been able to master even some of the most elementary tricks of life as a public person. One well-meaning rabbi's wife once told me I should practice learning the names of each group I ran into. If I were at a Women's Guild board meeting, I should jot down the names of those attending and count them out before I fell asleep at night—like sheep jumping over low stone walls. Right. I tried it and my sheep with congregants' faces all jumped over cliffs and disappeared.

As I'm edging my way out of The Hot Bagel (I've learned that the side of a room is a much better escape route than the middle) I see that Essie Sue has found someone worthy of her attention. She and Marla have joined a group of anorexically fashionable people, which I notice includes two of the ladies on my permanent list of avoidables. I'm almost at the door with my mind already in neutral, when I'm vaguely aware of something going on in the middle of the room. Or rather, I'm aware of something *not* going on.

There's this certain decibel level of crowd chatter that suddenly dies out. It takes me a few seconds to take in the scene. Almost in slow motion, I'm aware of people circling back from an open spot in the center of the room. The round space in the circle enlarges from doughnut size to wading pool. Tables are pushed back and people stand up and step backward.

It's eerie—like a huge, collective breath is being held. At first, there's only this hushed vacuum in the center of all the tables. The silence pushes out in concentric circles—then it breaks.

The next thing I know, someone is yelling, "She's

having some sort of seizure. Do something." I finally snap into focus. Without thinking what I'm doing, I look toward the table where Essie Sue and Marla had been seated. I head around pant legs and past big bottoms and endless chairs until I find the table. Marla is sprawled on the floor, and all I can think of is that she's "crazy dancing." One Halloween—years ago—Joshie had this witch toy connected to a pumpkin base. When a button at the base was pushed, the witch's segmented arms and legs twitched in all directions, and it bent and jerked at the waist. Joshie said to me, "I'm scared, Mommy. This witch is crazy dancing." That's what it reminds me of— Marla's upper body folded at the waist like that black and orange toy on its base.

I bend down to put a hand on Marla's shoulder when all of a sudden the stiff movements stop. Marla's rather pale gray eyes stare wide open and her mouth contorts like one of those photos halted in mid-action. The seizures just end—as if an immense shudder is passing through her body, leaving her a rigid stick figure.

That coordinated pantsuit is absorbing a trickle of pink pop dripping from a bottle on the table. She lies on her back, her left leg twisted at an outlandish angle. The bag of bagels spills at her side almost daintily. Her mouth is open, terribly crooked, and absolutely silent.

I've noticed details all my life, and I have really strong intuitions. I don't know what details make me so absolutely certain that Marla is dead. Maybe it's the absence of detail.

I hear somebody shout, "Call a doctor." A doctor I'm not, but she looks dead and I know this was no ordinary heart attack—I've seen too many heart attack victims.

I look up from her lying there and catch Milt's eye.
He's frozen behind his Formica counter. Then he gazes
beyond me and I turn around to see what he's looking
at. I've forgotten about Essie Sue. She's totally speechless—pale and just staring down at her sister on the
floor.

*I'm finally ready to try sleep, but I log on to the com-
puter* again just to see if Nan received my e-mail message. There's a short note from her:

E-mail from: Nan
To: Ruby
Subject: Riveted to the Spot

Don't dare forget to write me tomorrow with the
whole story—this sounds awful!
P.S. I know you, Ruby—Don't get too embroiled.

Embroiled? Me?

chapter 2

....

The usual after-funeral gathering turns out to be an after-memorial occasion, due to slight problems with the medical examiner's office. Events are, to say the least, out of order. Because of lingering questions as to the cause of Marla's death, an autopsy is being performed. With burial delayed, Essie Sue has insisted on today's memorial service at the Temple, near our small town square, followed by a service at the house.

The town of Eternal is topographically schizophrenic. The half where I live lies in the flat plain that leads eastward to the heart of the Old South in Louisiana and Mississippi. The other half, literally popping up from one street to the next, is a hilly, roller-coaster route to the Old West of New Mexico and Arizona. Ancient earthquakes had their way in this half of town, making for great views and soaring real estate.

Essie Sue lives amid the hills. Where else?

I walk into her crowded living room, dressed in my

tried-and-true basic black, and marvel once again at the resiliency that allows such a fast recovery—the life force is thumbing its nose at death. Just before the large memorial crowd filed out of the Temple, it was announced that the family would be "at home" at 401 Live Oak Drive after the service. Despite the suddenness and horror of Marla's fatal collapse, life goes on in the Margolis family. After the initial shock, Essie Sue has regained control of herself and the situation in all respects. The "at home" is at her home, to no one's surprise.

She's also written a home ceremony in memory of the deceased, but for the moment, bodies, not souls, are being fed. Two big glass bowls of herring in sour cream flank platters of fresh fleshy lox, sliced bagels, and rye bread. The cream cheese, plain and with chives, competes with layers of Cheddar and Swiss. Potato salad, marinated cucumber and tomato slices, fancy Jell-O molds, and hard-boiled eggs for life are crammed into every inch of the white-clothed table. A special side table is devoted to a huge coffee ring, brownies, and melt-in-your-mouth butter cookies dusted with powdered sugar.

I have a sudden craving for a dill pickle, and am just stuffing it into my mouth when Essie Sue appears, wearing an impeccable navy blue suit with white piping. Did I mention that she has an uncanny knack of catching me with my mouth full? Usually, it's just after I've acquired powdered sugar lips, so I guess I should count myself lucky it's just garlicky pickle juice this time. I napkin.

Essie Sue doesn't give me a chance for condolences.

"My loved ones made everything but the bagel platters," she tells me. "Your friend Milt catered those. I think he could have done a better job laying out the lox."

Not knowing how to answer, I take rare advantage of my former status as almost clergy.

"Shouldn't you be taking it easy at the family table, Essie Sue?" Tradition has it that, after burial, the mourners in the immediate family are spared the shoulder to shoulder, standing-room-only small talk, and are allowed to collapse and be waited on at a separate table, usually with the rabbi present for support. Here, there's been no burial, but Essie Sue has set the usual table. Dark rings have daringly escaped from beneath her eye makeup, and I know that somewhere under that commander in chief's armor lies vulnerability. I admit I've never seen it, but I'm convinced it's there.

"This service is at my house, so I don't have to sit at the table," she says, making up the rules as she goes. "I do think, though, since your husband's replacement hasn't been hired yet, it's inappropriate for you to stand around when you should be sitting with the family." Before I know it, I'm breaking bread between a great-aunt from St. Louis, who speaks only Yiddish, and Marla's daughter Glenda. I consider the aunt a stroke of luck. She doesn't expect any conversation, saving me the trouble of trying to converse with both sides at once—a trick of the trade I never learned.

I haven't seen Glenda in years. She's aged well—her tall, big-boned frame is as strong and straight as ever, and just as inhospitable to the graceful lines of fashion that occupied her mother and aunt. She and Milt Aboud of The Hot Bagel almost married when they were both at the university. Even though Glenda could have had her mother Marla's blessing with a fair amount of pushing, Aunt Essie Sue balked at the marriage. Rabbis from her congregation officiated only at marriages of Jews to Jews, Essie Sue said, and she was planning no wedding where one of those out-of-town clergymen had to be imported to do a mixed marriage.

Glenda inherited her gumption from her mother Marla, which meant of course that she caved in to her aunt Essie Sue's objections and decided not to marry Milt. Not having the courage to face him down, Glenda just grew increasingly distant until Milt finally said to hell with it. Milt didn't get around to telling Stu or me any of this for ages. He's been over Glenda for years, is happily married to an ex-Catholic, and says he never thinks about those earlier times much. Except, of course, whenever he sees Essie Sue, who's a customer in the bakery but doesn't speak to him.

Glenda seems truly in shock over her mother's death, and I find myself glad to be there for her.

"I wish your husband were still with us," she says. "I had a problem when I moved back to town two years ago, and I stopped by his study without an appointment. It was close to lunchtime. He took me to lunch and listened to me as if I were an old friend. I never forgot it. I could use some of his gentleness right now."

"I miss him, too. I do know he would have been devastated at what you're going through."

"I can't believe they haven't released Mother's body for burial yet," she says. "I didn't want just a memorial service. I wanted a funeral for her followed by burial. If we were Orthodox Jews, they'd have had to let us bury her right away."

Not wanting to even speculate on what might have

been the outcome of a clash between traditional Jewish practice and Texas bureaucracy, I decide to let that one pass. I reassure Glenda that her mother will be buried soon. Meanwhile, I'm surprised myself at the delay and wonder if she's heard anything. I plunge in.

"Did they decide this was some sort of seizure?"

"They don't know what it is. They're sending away samples to labs and all that. We can't find out anything."

"How's your aunt Essie Sue holding up?" I ask. "She and your mother were so close."

"I can't get much out of her. My uncle Hal has been a better shoulder to lean on. I don't know what's wrong with Aunt Essie Sue. She's got something to say about everything but this."

"She's probably in shock," I venture, at the exact moment Essie Sue comes over to our table looking like anything but a person in shock.

"Once we bury Marla," she says, "I have two things on my agenda. It's a disgrace we had to bring in a rabbi to do the service. I want the Rabbinical Selection Committee to make a selection right away from our three finalists. We waited a year to let people get over your late husband's accident, and we're now six months past our deadline. The other thing on my agenda . . ."

She's now pushing too many buttons. Memorials are hard enough for me these days, since the hit-and-run that killed Stu. And the last thing I want to know is Essie Sue's agenda. I hug Glenda, make my good-byes, and tell Essie Sue I'll have to hear about it all another day.

The borrowed rabbi rings the doorbell just in the nick of time. I need to go home.

"But you have to stay for the service," Essie Sue demands.

"I'm not the rabbi," I say. I'm out the door.

E-mail from: Ruby
To: Nan
Subject: *Mourning Becomes Eternal*

Tried to sleep but I can't, so here I am. I told you about the medical examiner holding the body, yes? I have no idea what that's all about. The memorial service was at temple today, and then I spent an upsetting afternoon at the Margolises', which I won't go into right now because I need to talk about something else besides death.

On a lighter subject, remember when we were wheeling our babies together here twenty years ago and we used to roar with laughter over some of the more pretentious souls Stu and I had to deal with? Well, I have a story for you. I did tell you, didn't I, that they've finally gotten their act together here and are interviewing rabbis? Even though there were plenty of women on the placement list, the finalists are all men. Surprise, surprise. They're down to three, and although I let the congregational officers talk me into being on the temple board during this transition period, I tried to stay away from the selection process. I did attend the "wish list" session before they started interviewing. Big mistake.

No one at the meeting was overly interested in scholarship, but the powers that be seemed to be falling into three groups. Since Stu as rabbi was more interested in people than in pronouncements or decibel levels, Essie Sue Margolis's contingent now wants something different. The key word here is *charisma*. He should also *look* like a rabbi, whatever that means. If he's *charismatic* enough and doesn't stoop to the people like Stu did, the congregants will apparently rise up to his level, attend services more frequently, and respond to fund-raisers.

These are good people, Nan, and they're my people. I'm very much one of them, which is why this process bothers me so much. I just wish they'd stop letting themselves be led around by the nose. My worst fear is that they'll get what they wish for and end up with someone powerful and condescending to boot.

And speaking of boots, Brother Copeland, Brotherhood president and grandson of the founding family, wants someone "with tradition"—that doesn't mean Jewish tradition—it means hopefully the candidate's ancestors put the first stone in a temple building somewhere in Texas in the nineteenth century. Looks are not a priority; being a good ol' boy is.

I'm hoping the temple president, Turner Goldman, wins out. He's looking for values. Of course, they all say they are—it's just that the president knows how to prioritize. He'd like to see how the candidates relate to teenagers—not because their concerns are more important than the other congregants', but because kids can spot a phony ten miles off.

chapter
3

....

Milt and I stalk the aisles of the Computer Village fax section after closing time at the bakery. We've driven from Eternal to an Austin shopping center, just to argue the merits of plain-vanilla faxes with those sporting more bells and whistles, deliberately trying not to mention what is uppermost in our minds.

"Why would I want to pay an extra seventy-five dollars for something that can send more than ten pages at a time?" Milt fidgets with a fax phone attached to the side of a particularly complicated number pad. "I'm not sending any faxes—I'm just receiving lunch orders."

"That feature was two faxes ago, Milt. Now I'm asking you to look at the 'One Touch' button on this machine. You're not paying attention."

"What I have paid attention to is the fact that this place is totally deserted. Have you seen one store employee other than the cashier since we came in here? Jesus, we could walk away with everything in here that's not nailed down. If I ran my business this way, I'd be broke in a month."

I stop at the end of the aisle. "This obviously isn't working. Neither of us can think of anything but Marla, so let's just go sit somewhere and hash it all out for the umpteenth time. Okay?"

Milt rubs his chin, scratching the heavy stubble that defies even two shaves a day. "I know you didn't have a lot of time this week, Ruby. I hate to bring you here and then have to come back. But you're right—I'm no good tonight. Let's head outside. I saw a bench."

As we push some newspapers aside and settle ourselves to face the other side of the shopping strip, I realize how really awful Milt looks. I wonder if I look as bad. If the days since Marla's death have been a nightmare for me, I can imagine how they've been for Milt. He's sitting head down, with his hands clasped behind his neck. I can hardly hear him.

"Glenda and I were really tight in college," he says. "We almost got engaged. I felt a special bond for years after, even though we broke up before graduation. Believe me, I didn't have so many women that I could afford to forget any of them that easily. She moved away after graduation and I didn't see her for years until she and her mother Marla moved back here a couple of years ago. Marla was nice to me, too, before her sister Essie Sue got hold of her. When I remember how Marla looked the other day, I—I don't know what."

"Have you thought of closing up for a few days?"

"Close up? It feels like we're closed up already. The crowd is congregating outside, not inside. Nobody comes in there—at least not to eat. What they do is to run in, go to the cash register on the other side from where Marla was, order a bag of bagels, and run out. My head baker says I ought to be glad they come in at all. People don't like to be reminded that someone's died of a stroke or heart attack right where they're standing."

"It won't last, Milt. They'll forget about it." I'm hoping I look more optimistic than I feel. I had been plunged into depression from the moment I saw Marla lying on the bakery floor. It brought back everything I had imagined about Stu's death but had not been able to witness. Not only did I feel weighted down by the death of this woman I had talked to and even touched as we stood arm to arm in line, but the sadness was doubled by the memories it evoked of my own husband's sudden death over a year ago.

Stu had been the victim of a hit-and-run—the car was never located, and the emotional wounds of the shock had been left open to heal in haphazard fashion, without order or reason. Imagining how he looked as he lay in the street, knocked from a pedestrian crossing near the Temple at nine o'clock on a spring night, was far worse than having been able to see and comfort him—or at least to have tried. Any death since then had started a mini vortex churning in my stomach. But this one—so abrupt, so horrifying—was especially hard to accept.

Because I was one of the last people that day to have spoken to Marla, I had waited, even before I was asked, to speak to the paramedics. They had come quickly, and it was no surprise to me that Marla was pronounced dead almost immediately. There was simply no question in my mind that the once-attractive woman lying between the tables was dead.

"How did you know, too, Milt?" I'm vaguely aware that my question is a disconnected one, but I expect Milt to answer it, anyway. The exchange is characteristic of all our recent conversations. We have become like fox-hole buddies—totally in sync with each other but just as totally out of sync with ordinary mortals.

"I don't know how I knew she was dead. My counter's raised up enough so that I get a pretty good view of the whole place. Maybe something about her position on the floor, maybe her face—maybe just reading your face. I've had a couple of other scares over the years, but the paramedics never got there so fast before. When in the hell do you think we'll know what she died of?"

I have no idea, and say so. The late sunset finally darkens our corner of the shopping strip, and although there is no way the air could have become less muggy in so short a time, the absence of light gives the illusion of coolness. We sit on the bench, looking at our shoes like chastened children, but feeling woefully, regrettably adult.

Milt had been Stu's friend, and later, mine. Stu had discovered the bakery years ago, and looked forward to lingering over coffee and schmoozing with Milt about family in New York. Milt's family had been in the bagel business for three generations, though he wasn't in touch with them. Stu loved telling stories of the old days when his grandfather and uncles had been part of the bagel trade. Stu had felt especially close to them and to his own childhood days when he talked to Milt.

Stopping by Milt's bakery was one of the few bright spots for me in the months after Stu's death. This man knew of Stu's family, knew Stu in his most relaxed and unprofessional role, and provided a safe haven. Since the recent remodeling of the business, of course, that safe haven has changed from relaxed to frantic. Only in this town would the Jews flock to a Lebanese bagel bakery and totally ignore the competition—Kulberg's Deli— run by Jewish expatriates from Brooklyn. There's a reason for that. Milt has a magic touch with food, while his competition's matzo balls are like rocks sinking in warm water. Or worse. The Kulbergs' collective cultural memory apparently faded when they crossed the Texas border.

Milt himself hasn't changed since we first met. He's still plainspoken and, as he often says, unimpressed by the clergy—a trait I'm especially grateful for, since it means I can be a person with him and not a parental stand-in. This last characteristic is one I look for in any of my close friendships. Life is difficult enough without having friends who feel they must be on their best behavior whenever they're in your company.

When I told a new friend once that Stu and I had just made up from a fight, the woman asked, "You mean you two argue?" It took me a while to absorb that one. Apparently, the general public just didn't think we were quite human. As the years passed, I began to realize, as I e-mailed to Nan, that "Most people don't want God at their New Year's Eve party." Still, I've managed, and the friends with the guts to jump the hurdle were, of course, exactly those I wanted and needed. Milt is one of those friends.

"Do you want to go back in and see if you can find the fax of your dreams? At least it's air conditioned inside." I get up from the bench and unstick my shirt from my damp back.

"I have to see if a flour delivery came in for tonight's shift. Let's put this off for now. If we go back to Eternal, we can have some iced coffee in the bakery. I'll make it up to you. My mind's on Marla's death."

"Well, the whole purpose of this shopping trip was to have a diversion, so you certainly don't need to apologize. I needed one, too."

We drive quickly down the freeway, named for the original Missouri Pacific railroad beside it, leaving behind the new suburbs of high-tech Austin and entering the laid-back central area which had never wanted to leave the sixties. Janis Joplin's favorite hangout goes on without her, and the hippie musicians' paradise—half commune, half performance hall—has disappeared, never to really be replaced; but the quirky, unconventional spirit of those days still remains. Two hundred people can still be mobilized to confront the county with banners when it threatens to remove as an eyesore the flock of painted flamingos gracing an empty lot.

The little town of Eternal was once larger than Austin, but the railroad passed it by, leaving it out to pasture just south of the city. Newcomers now think of it as a suburb in itself, though it's really the distilled essence of what Austin used to be. Younger people in Eternal are even more funky than in Austin, if that's possible. In most cases, this means torn jeans instead of jeans.

We still have the old town square, though its centerpiece, the dark red county courthouse, is now the largest Methodist church in town. The church pays for the upkeep of the park, and Eternal gets to enjoy it. Most of the good shopping is gone now—up the freeway to the city, but that's only twenty minutes away. The Temple is downtown—two blocks from the square, near The Hot Bagel. A bagel bakery run by the son of a Lebanese immigrant without an ounce of Jewish blood is totally plausible here.

"What do you think the old-time purists would have said about raisin bagels?" I dip one into a glass of iced coffee. "Or worse, the new jalapeño bagels you just instigated for a Southwest touch."

"Feh!" Milt answers.

"What do you know from 'feh'? They would have dismissed you as a goy."

"A goy, yes. But a goy with New York roots. So do you want to take any bets on who's more of a goy—a dyed-in-the-wool ex–New Yorker whose mother gave him a salami end to teethe on, or an East Texas ex-rebbitzen who grew up on collard greens? I don't even think you're bona fide Jewish."

"Yes I am, wiseguy. Both sides. My grandfather came to this country through the port of Galveston and became a traveling peddler. His hometown was where the horse died. The buggy became his first store and our family has lived there ever since."

"Amazing. How in the hell did you survive the Yiddish fishbowl?"

"I was a quick study. I learned more Yiddish expressions the first year of marriage than I had known my whole life before. I used to keep a Jewish cookbook by the telephone. Whenever one of our congregants called up to ask how to make matzo ball soup or for my favorite gefilte fish recipe, I'd quick give her a recipe from the book. But to tell you the truth, I never did get the hang of seasoning anything that didn't have a little East Texas/West Louisiana tang to it."

I'm glad to see Milt has brightened a bit. I'm almost hesitant to bring up the subject of Marla, so I stir my coffee silently while Milt phones the man he calls his "flour connection."

"Get your ass down here soon, Al, or my bakers'll have nothing to do." He waves me down when I start toward my purse. "Stay for a minute," he says, putting his hand over the mouthpiece.

Milt leans forward on the big baker's table, which forms the centerpiece of the kitchen, and pulls a carton of lox-flavored cream cheese toward me.

"Don't tempt me," I say, sliding it back to him. "You know my attraction for bagels and lox—especially after a week like this."

"So indulge. I can't think of a better time than when you're stressed out."

"My goal is to relieve my stress by playing with my computer instead of my food. Besides, I don't see you eating any bagels."

"After years in the business, some bakers think of our bagels like part of the furniture or the wallpaper. Believe it or not, I still love 'em, so I need to really watch it. I can test for an off-taste when I need to, but I don't eat them very often." Milt leans over to grab the phone. "That has to be Al again," he said, catching the phone on the second ring.

I munch on a rye bagel, sans cream cheese. A couple of minutes go by before I realize all is quiet on Milt's end of the conversation. I look up and see him scribbling furiously on loose, multicolored message papers, pulling new ones from a square Lucite box, and scattering full ones all around him. The color drains from his face.

"Do you want something bigger to write on?" I mouth. He shakes his head, still plucking pages from the holder. Finally, he speaks.

"Can we make it tonight?" he asks the caller. "I won't get any sleep anyway, and I have to get back here at four in the morning." I become alarmed—Milt looks so stricken. After a couple of "okays," he hangs up and stares before him.

"That was the precinct. I wanted them to come over tonight, but they're coming over here in the morning to talk to me."

"What about?" I feel my stomach beginning to knot.

"The autopsy report came back," he says. "It's cyanide poisoning. They found the poison inside her, and the bagel she was eating was full of cyanide. The bagel I gave her."

chapter
4

....

E-mail from: Nan
To: Ruby
Subject: *What Gives?*

   So are you telling me she was murdered? Surely Milt's
not a suspect. What happened when they brought him
in? Did you tell him to take a lawyer with him, or would
that seem suspicious? Are there any strange characters
working for him? You didn't get on here yesterday, and
I almost phoned you. I'm not asking too many questions,
am I? I know you'd feel the same way if this thing were
reversed, Ruby, so *write!*

....

E-mail from: Ruby
To: Nan
Subject: *Don't Bust a Gut*

You? Ask too many questions? You're joking, right? And by the way, weren't you the one warning *me* not to get too involved? Frankly, I'm glad I have you to pour out to. I can't make Milt too nervous, so I'm watching what I say to him.

Today the police went to the bakery and interviewed all the employees. Last I heard, they were also getting ready to conduct a search of the whole place. But I'm getting too far ahead of myself, so I'll try to answer your questions. First, Milt went in for questioning yesterday without a lawyer. Grace—that's his wife—took off work and went with him. They talked to him for a couple of hours, and of course were very interested in his connection with Marla's daughter, Glenda. He told them about the almost-engagement, the breakup, and not seeing her for all those years until she came back to Eternal to live. He also told them he only saw her now as a customer and didn't know that much about her life. He said he'd have a much bigger reason to hold a grudge against Essie Sue than Marla, if it came down to that.

They finished with him by late morning, but warned him they'd be coming to the bakery to do a thorough search. Remember, the day Marla died nobody thought it was murder. Now it's a whole different story. Grace and the kids are worried to death because the police seem interested in Milt, and he's losing sleep because nobody's coming in to eat. I'm telling you, Nan, I'm staying close to this as long as Milt's involved.

Next question you asked—as for strange characters, you have to be a little odd to be in the bakery business in the first place. I mean, how many people like to start the day at four in the morning? But yeah—a couple of them are a little strange. The chief baker, Gus Stamish, looks Ichabod Crane-ish, with a skinny body and an elongated head that's bent forward I swear like a croissant. His people skills are shall we say nonexistent, but Milt says Gus knows what he's doing as long as he stays behind the counter. Way behind the counter.

The other weird one isn't making a career from bagels—he's a Ph.D. candidate from the U—Bradley Axelrod. He doesn't have a life that I can tell—just the books and the bagels, in that order. He supports himself by working full-time in the bakery while he's writing his thesis on vectors. That's all I know—vectors. He's thin, has a glassy-eyed look, and aside from a five, six, and seven o'clock shadow, which he tries to cover with talcum powder, nothing stands out, appearance-wise.

Milt's other help is temporary, mostly college kids. One other full-timer is . . . whoops—phone ringing on the other line—I'll send and sign off for a minute.

· ·

E-mail from: Ruby
To: Nan
Subject: *The Worst*

That was Milt. The police had searched all the trash containers inside and outside the bakery. They found a small vial containing a few drops of almond flavoring, heavily laced with cyanide. Milt's fingerprints were the only ones on the vial. Of course, they would be, because he's the only one who flavors the dough. Not that this is any help. As I said, he flavors the dough. This is getting more awful by the minute.

I'm outa here.

....

E-mail from: Ruby
To: Nan
Subject: *Continued*

Milt, Grace, and their two oldest kids were already confabbing in the back room of the bakery when I got there. I told them I'd be glad to take a turn working if it turned out Milt needed the time off. Grace said they *would* need me if Milt wasn't there. It's such a *meshuganah* business with the odd hours and the chaos at lunch and dinnertime. The number one topic on our agenda was getting a good lawyer for Milt. This is an area where I knew I could be helpful. Turner Goldman, president of the Temple, was my first pick. He has an excellent reputation as a defense lawyer, but he's so busy he usually sends new clients to his associates. I picked up the phone and got through to him—a clergy perk. He's meeting with Milt tonight, hopefully to be prepared for whatever's going to happen, but part of the deal for taking Milt as a client was that I'd promise to attend the temple board meeting this week.

Don't expect too much news from me for a day or two, okay? I know I'll be racing—like they say gruesomely in these parts—like a chicken with its head cut off.

chapter
5

....

Whenever I cross the threshold of the Temple these days, my chest feels heavy, as if I'd just gulped down bad Tex-Mex. I used to love walking in here—it was home to me. Now I feel so lonely. Most of this emotion, I know, is sadness for Stu, but the other part is leftover anxiety which, like jet lag, reaches out and pulls my steps backward even as I'm going forward. And like jet lag, it's not real, yet it is real. I'm also feeling bottomed-out because I sense in my bones Milt's in for a long ordeal—even *with* Turner Goldman's help.

I'm late. The Kaufman clock with the gilded Hebrew numbers is just chiming eight, and the meeting was set for seven-thirty. I hang my jacket in the Goldberg cloak-room, just off the Blumberg social hall. Jewish fund-raising is not nameless. Actually, there's one exception to that—the name of the Temple itself. The town of Eternal has always called it simply "the Temple," and, like everything else, there's a reason for it. Most synagogues bear familiar Hebraic names—not simply "the Temple." Our building sprang into being in 1925 as the result of one major beneficent act. Miss Rita Fenstermeister, last surviving daughter of a family that made its fortune in hat manufacturing, left her entire estate to the fledgling building fund begun by Eternal's fifty Jewish families, who had outgrown their meeting place in each other's homes.

The bequest was large enough to finance the whole project. But like the old joke about the Plotnick diamond, which brought a blessing for the woman who received it (the blessing of the jewel's great worth) and a curse (Plotnick came with it), the Fenstermeister *1925* bequest came with a price. The will stated categorically that the Temple bear its benefactor's name. Temple Fenstermeister? *Oy vay*. But Jewish ingenuity came to the rescue. Not for nothing did the congregational lawyers carry in their genes the heritage of generations of scholars used to dealing with the intricacies of the Talmud. They had a plan. On Dedication Day in 1927 all eyes looked up to the engraved stonework above the big double doors of the entrance to the sanctuary. The name, in elaborate curlicue script, was almost impossible to make out, but there it was—*Temple Rita*. After all, that *was* her name, and nothing in the will had specified first or last.

The congregation and the town had spent the last seventy or so years conveniently ignoring the name. Even the stationery simply said, "The Temple." Stu and I literally lost it when we first read his employment contract listing the full name of the congregation, and I can never walk under the nameplate without thinking of the forgotten Miss Rita, who's undoubtedly turning over in her grave.

I tiptoe into the boardroom, hoping to sit behind the others lined up around the big oak table, but Turner lifts his hand and waggles me over to the corner beside him. It's better than sitting next to Essie Sue on the other side. The meeting is progressing with its usual style and panache. Buster Copeland, chairman of the Maintenance Committee, has the floor.

"Toilet paper, ladies and gentlemen. Toilet paper must be addressed, and we're using too much of it. I leave the spirituality to others. There are those of us who only stoop and serve."

"*Stand* and serve," someone pipes up.

"I'd say stooping's more to the point. Standing don't waste as much paper." That's Buster's brother Brother. "Buster, when are you gonna get over 1962 when you were treasurer of the frat house at the university? This here ain't a fraternity meeting." Brother and Buster are only a year apart in age, but they have identical graying goatees and have never shed the open-collared Oxford blue shirts, chinos, and boots of their college days. They're far from twin-like, though. The more elevated Buster's language, the more ordinary Brother gets.

"I beg to differ," Buster says. "This temple has to learn some fiscal self-control. I turned the frat house around in one year."

"So are you suggesting we hold it in?"

"That's not the point. My plan is to switch to one of the thousand sheets a roll brands. Softness is expensive, and it's about time we learned it."

"Man, don't you know they'll just use more paper with that thin stuff?"

"Not true if we have a campaign to educate. Let 'em use the expensive stuff at home." Buster is adamant. "Remember that party with the sorority where Marla's daughter Glenda brought her boyfriend Milt and he wanted to 'TP' the rec room because he was mad at— oops—Sorry, Essie Sue."

Turner's wry voice comes through the fray. "Before we end up with Buster here as chairman of the Education Committee where he can do some real damage, why don't we table this discussion?"

"Point of order, point of order!" Buster yells. I'm thinking Turner's got another thought coming if he imagines he'll get rid of Buster that easily. And these guys say it's women who are obsessed with trivia.

Ignoring Turner's gaveling, Buster pulls out a chart from under the table.

"Omygod, he's graphed it," Brother says.

"Microsoft chart, ladies and gentlemen." A beaming Buster points to vertical rows of tiny toilet paper rolls bearing dollar signs intersecting horizontal rows of—

"Is that library books?"

"Yep, Brother, I've figured out how many books we can buy for our temple library next year if we switch to my new Restroom Economy Plan. Call the question. Call the question, Mr. Chairman. There's a motion still standing."

"That's about all that's still standing," Brother says. "Let's have a vote, Mr. Chairman. You know damn well you're not getting him to sit down after he's done all this work."

Buster's Restroom Economy Plan passes fourteen to two. I try to think of other things—a habit I'm good at in these situations. Essie Sue Margolis, glaring throughout the discussion, is no doubt already making plans to carry her own Charmin. Fortunately for Buster, her mind seems to be preoccupied with other matters. She raises her hand at the call for new business, and rises without waiting to be recognized.

My mind continues on automatic pilot as Essie Sue introduces her new business. Like driving on the freeway while your thoughts are a million miles away—zoning out can work for a while, but the experience is jarring. Suddenly I come to attention; surely I couldn't be hearing what I'm hearing. She wants to erect a statue of her murdered sister near the entrance steps?

"Ladies and gentlemen of the board. All of you know what a tremendous contribution of time and service my late sister Marla made to this congregation. Now that she has gone to her untimely reward, the very least we can do is to honor her memory in an extraordinary way. I have contacted the renowned sculptor Carlo Bellberg, who is prepared to erect a life-sized image of the biblical figure Queen Esther, using my sister Marla's likeness as his model. The statue will be carved from the finest marble available and will weigh approximately five thousand pounds."

"You're kidding, right?" Turner's face is incredulous.

"You know I never joke, Turner. And I'm shocked that you would react to my family's time of grief so lightly. In case you're concerned, the temple budget will not be involved. The Margolis family will contribute half the cost, with the remaining half to be obtained by fund-raising. I have no doubt that the heart of this community will come through for us."

"Fund-raising? You expect fund-raising, yet?" Buster is on his feet. "And Marla as Queen Esther? Tell me I'm dreaming."

"May I remind you that my sister's murderer is still at large? A little sympathy is what I would have expected." Essie Sue is staring him down, but Buster's not moving.

Turner is trying to keep control. "You have all our sympathy, Essie Sue. But this is a big deal here."

"Is this new business or is it not? Mrs. Parliamentarian, can we hear from you? If there's no more discussion, call the question."

The parliamentarian is Essie Sue's sister-in-law. Essie Sue is a woman with a mission, and I suddenly realize she's probably done her homework. She's responsible for recruiting most of these people to the board.

"Whaddaya mean, no discussion? Point of order," Buster shouts.

"Time out!" I recognize the voice of the immediate past president.

"This ain't a football game." Brother's red in the face.

"We should call for a vote on this right now," Essie Sue says, without waiting for the parliamentarian to answer the question she just asked her.

Turner makes another try. I whisper to him that he's lucky his trial experience has thickened his skin.

"Oh, yeah?" he whispers back. "I'll take a capital murder case any day over dealing with these *meshuganahs*. Accepting this presidency has been the biggest sacrifice I've ever made for the Jewish people." He stands up.

"Okay, folks. This is the way it's gonna be. I'm tabling this discussion for what I thought was going to be the main topic tonight—a report from the Selection Committee on the progress made for a new rabbi. Don't tell me anything's more important than that."

I look across the table and see a half smile on Essie Sue's face. That's a shock.

"Excellent idea," she says. "We'll leave this decision on the statue up to the new rabbi. It will be first on my list of prime questions for the prospectives."

I can't suppress a groan. Just what the new rabbi needs when he hits town. On the other hand, if this does become part of the selection process, at least he can't say he wasn't warned.

Turner has appointed himself head of the Selection Committee, claiming he didn't dare put the job in anyone else's hands. A good idea, but he's still only a minority of one.

"Members of the board, three committee members, including myself, will speak for the rabbis we've been investigating."

Investigating? I'm already shuddering.

"I've decided to take presidential prerogative and tell you first about the rabbi I was assigned to."

"You assigned yourself," Essie Sue reminded him.

"Whatever. I'm very much impressed with this fellow, and he reminds me somewhat of our late Rabbi Stu. Like him, he's someone you can feel comfortable with. His name is David Burney, and of course you know that the entire committee attended services at his present congregation. He and his wife invited us to his home one of the nights we were there, and treated us as if they'd known us all their lives. His congregants love him . . ."

"Of course they love him," Ed Levy chipped in. "He's not going to let you near the ones that don't."

"Let me finish, Ed. You know these visits have to be kept quiet, just as with any job interview. Anyway, I liked him. He's well versed in all the Jewish teachings he's supposed to be well versed in, but aside from that, he's an all-round nice guy. The kids take to him, too. I could tell by the way they looked at him. They all call him Rabbi David."

"What was the wife like? You know how important that is," says Essie Sue's sister-in-law, the parliamentarian.

I grab this opportunity. "Why don't I leave early and give all of you the chance to really get into this without any embarrassment," I say as earnestly as possible.

"Oh no you don't," Turner whispers. "A deal is a deal."

"We're not embarrassed," Essie Sue assures me, and we all know she's right. Sensitivity is not a long suit on this board. I resign myself to the evening.

"His wife is very nice. She's a stockbroker."

"Will she have enough time for the congregation?" the bake sale chairman asks. "Why can't we get somebody who's a full-time homemaker?"

Turner rises again. "Hello? This is the nineties, remember? And besides, if she's a full-time homemaker, how can she be the full-time professional rabbi's wife with no pay you're looking for?"

Brother stands up. "Sit down, Turner. It's getting late, and we need our turn, too."

Turner sits down. "Okay, I guess I've taken enough time for now."

"My rabbi is just what this congregation needs." Brother seems reenergized—this doesn't bode well for my getting out of here before midnight. I notice that Essie Sue, looking bored, too, is wearing black—but definitely Neiman Marcus–brand mourning robes. I wonder if she had all this black in her closet or if she made a special shopping trip. I hear she's furious with Turner Goldman for taking Milt's case. In her mind, there could certainly be no more suitable villain than Milt, since she's held a grudge against him ever since he had the effrontery to aspire to her as an aunt-in-law. According to Turner, she's been bad-mouthing Milt to the police. The one thing she doesn't know yet is that I arranged for Turner to take Milt as a client, and I'm not relishing that revelation.

Brother is finishing up the pitch for his rabbi. "And in conclusion, ladies and gents, I want to paint this picture for you. There we were, at the Jews and the Old West Conference, and the rabbi they brought in to conduct the service was standing in front of us, wearing the most beautiful pair of eelskin cowboy boots you ever saw in your life. The Star of David was etched on 'em, and that rabbi, Rabbi Grady Greenberg, told me he almost never takes 'em off his feet. Think of what that says about a man. I had tears in my eyes when he called for a moment of silence for . . ."

"Spare us." Essie Sue's expression is dark. "You've been talking for twenty minutes—I clocked it, and if our illustrious president can't keep control of this meeting, I can."

"But I haven't told yet about the tall tale he told for a sermon. He's a hellava good preacher," Brother says before yielding the floor.

I ask Turner why we can't do this search more professionally, like the larger congregations do.

"Because they have more families and can afford it," he tells me—apparently satisfied that this is an answer. Turner's my friend, but even he only half-listens to my opinions. Whatever I say is still considered semiprofessional—therefore, not a *real* point of view. I lean over to press my case with him, when Essie Sue shushes me.

"Nothing I've heard yet has impressed me," she says. "But I found a thirty-eight-year-old young man we'll all want."

Essie Sue has that determined glint in her eyes. She's off and running. "Ask Rabbi Kevin Kapstein what *he'd* like to be called and he says, 'Call me Rabbi Kapstein,' " she says. "Now, that's dignity.

"He has light brown hair, worn straight and longish in back—elegant, I'd say. He's a bit stocky, very short in stature, but he's distinguished. He says his wife never ever refers to him by his first name—he's got her trained. She *likes* calling him rabbi. If somebody's cheeky enough to call on the phone and ask for Kevin, she says, 'The rabbi will speak to you in a moment.' And that's no matter who's calling—even another rabbi. This man has his priorities straight. His dignity is the prime consideration of his family and himself."

We're all riveted. Essie Sue has that knack. "The rabbi's wife was out of town when we visited, but he says she's a tall blonde, twenty-nine years old. His nick-name for her, which the congregation has adopted, is Kitselah. Rabbi Kapstein tells me that Kitselah is very protective of his time, and she is respectful and even worshipful of him when she sits before him in the front pew, where she's often carried into the emotional heights by his words. She tells people he is spectacular. Can we ask for more?"

"Well, yeah," Buster breaks in, "we can ask for more, Essie Sue. He sounds like he's got a rod—"

"I'm just getting started." Essie Sue withers Buster with a steely look, and goes on. "What do we want—chummy or charismatic? Friendly or fiery? Darling or dynamic? The answer is obvious, and it's about time."

"All this dynamism for a mere three hundred and twenty-five families?" Turner whispers to me, looking at his watch. "Why don't the big temples want him?"

"I can't wait to meet this miraculous wife who mirrors the rabbi's glory," I whisper back. "Arrogance Are Us."

"It's eleven-thirty at night," Turner announces.

Even Essie Sue can't fight the clock. We finally table everything and pour out of the building—limp, listless, and in my case, livid. I'm seeing Milt tomorrow. He's gonna owe me big.

chapter
6

....

E-mail from: Ruby
To: Nan
Subject: *Write Me Back as Soon as You Get This*

I'm scared. Maybe the mug of Celis I just stuck in the freezer will calm me down—I hope so. Part of the calming down process is that I have to tell this from the very beginning, so hold on.

Milt was arrested today for the murder of Marla Solomon—not even Turner Goldman could prevent it, although Turner's working nonstop on the case and tells me it's far from a done deal. There was no time to really digest all this, since I had to go to the bakery as soon as I got the call. I'd promised Milt and Grace to fill in and keep an eye on things if this happened.

First of all, I was surprised we did any business today, period. Milt had been so disappointed in the turnout during the days after the murder that I'd assumed the place was a graveyard. Which it was, I guess, but no pun intended. The crowds are way down with almost no sit-down business, but we did have a decent day's sales, which convinces me more than ever that, business-wise, The Hot Bagel is filling a real gap in this town. There's nothing else as good anywhere around, and people are apparently hooked on the bagels.

I've had to turn down some fees because of all this chaos with the murder, but freelance computer consulting hasn't been all that great lately, anyway. I've got to make the decision to work for one of the hotshot companies in Austin if I'm going to support myself and help keep Josh in college. Forgive the digression, but this comes to mind because of something I don't think I told you. A couple of months ago, Milt asked if I'd consider going into business with him. I laughed, imagining what some of the temple cronies would say about the former rabbi's wife selling bagels, but I didn't give it serious thought. The head baker, Gus, who was at the counter at the time, said the idea was hilariously funny, which, of course, made me want to take it seriously. The beauty of it would be that with some income from this investment, I could still do the consulting part-time and be my own boss. Helping out Milt this week is giving me a sample of what running The Hot Bagel would be like.

As you know, I can't be in a place five minutes without wanting to fix it. Besides the fact that the bakery is woefully unautomated, the decor certainly leaves something to be desired. If I were involved, I'd have some of the baking areas glassed in and more accessible to the patrons—a substantive atmosphere, you might say, like some of the local microbreweries. Now, the bakers are stuck way back and isolated. Since Milt insists that the whole process be scrupulously clean, he might as well make a virtue of that. He has nothing to hide.

I'd also bring in some books, newspapers, and magazines, and make the seating more comfortable. And of course, we haven't even gotten into the ways the business could be computerized. Now that I think of it, Milt's lucky I *didn't* take him seriously. He's technophobic, and he thinks the place looks just right the way it is.

The day went fine, except for one crank call asking if we only cooked "Jew food." Carol Sealy, the assistant cashier, was too clueless to deal with it, so I got on the phone. Despite my first answer that if the caller meant Jewish food, we weren't a kosher restaurant, but we did offer deli-style sandwiches, the guy kept up the sarcasm. I really seethe when I run into an anti-Semite. I finally told him that although the whole world enjoys bagels these days, we'd be happy to sell ours to everybody else, and he shouldn't hurry in.

I spent most of my time boosting the morale of the bakers and counter workers, who are all worried they'll be out of jobs with Milt gone. Before closing time tonight, I decided to have a brainstorming session with the employees to see if I could learn anything new. The police had questioned all of them to see if there was any connection with Marla. My idea was to work on the possibility that someone wanted to put Milt away for some reason. Everything's too pat—leftover cyanide? Gimme a break. Why wouldn't he throw it away somewhere else? Anyway, I just told the bakery crew I wanted to get everybody together to see if we could think of any way to help Milt.

We almost had a fight. Bradley Axelrod, the math student, accused Carol of being a disloyal shit because she's ready to quit. When she intimated that where there's smoke there's fire, Bradley almost took after her. That quiet little guy's got a temper.

Then head baker Gus got into it by teasing Carol, in that snide, sarcastic way he has, for having a crush on Milt. Gus claimed Carol was angry at Milt because he's never shown any interest in her. I wanted to continue the discussion a little longer, but I was afraid I'd seem over-eager to play detective, and then have them suspicious of me. I called it quits and sent them all home after both Gus and Carol started asking why we needed this meeting anyway.

Now comes the creepy part. I'm gonna try to tell you this step-by-step just as it happened. I fool around in the bakery until around nine o'clock. After I put the day's cash in the money box for Grace, check the back door, and make some accounting notes Milt asked me to keep, I lock the front door and head for my car in the lot across the street. Luckily, I have nothing in my hands—just a fanny pack around my waist.

You know Village Street on a summer night—on any night at this time, for that matter. This burb is deserted. To the right of The Hot Bagel is Strand Cleaners, closed. To the left is the Tae Kwon Do Parlor, closed. The Thirty Flavors that used to be open until ten moved to the North End shopping center. I'm the only one on the street probably for a mile down, but just like my mother taught me, I still look both ways before jaywalking to my car.

I swear I see absolutely nothing coming. Where it does

come from, I don't know—maybe swerving out of the driveway of the cleaners next door. All I know is it wasn't there one minute ago. I do admit that because the street is so deserted, my looking both ways is more gesture and habit than actual seeing. My mind is usually on something else, and tonight is no different. It's dark, and the streetlight all the way at the end of Village Street is no help.

The horrible part is I don't see the car. At all. I don't know what saves me, unless it's the fact I used to be the best dodgeball player in school—I could move it when I had to, and now I have to. This missile comes toward me. I don't see shape, I don't see color, I don't see anything but *big*. And it goes without saying I don't see the driver. I don't even consciously know it *is* a vehicle—it's just there. I jump backward to avoid it—my best playground dodges were backward and slightly to the side and I guess my body remembers. If I'd had my hands full, I would have never been free to jump that fast.

I fall backward and lie there for—for not very long. I'm not knocked out—my senses are on overdrive, and I scramble to my feet as soon as the dizzy feeling leaves. I don't hear a car roaring off. I hear nothing. And when I look up and down the street, I see nothing.

That's it. That's the way it was, Nan. I drove home a couple of hours ago. I needed to take a shower and lie down. Then I needed to write you. Don't worry—only my shoulder hurts and my elbow is scraped. I definitely didn't land on my head and have no concussion. I know this hasn't hit me yet, but I do have a kind of doomsday feeling I can't shake and can't explain. Do you think it's just the shock? It could have been any speeder and probably a drunk, but why do people have to be so vile as to not stop?

....

E-mail from: Nan
To: Ruby
Subject: *Go Directly to the Doctor: Do Not Pass Go*

What's killing me here, Ruby, is that I know you're not going to listen to me about the doctor or the emergency room. I'd almost settle for getting you to go tomorrow except that in cases of concussion, *as you well know*, you really shouldn't go to sleep without having someone there to awaken you from time to time. And of course, if you went to the emergency room and had it checked out now, you could go home and sleep without being awakened because a concussion had already been ruled out. See?

Maybe I'll just try to keep you up all night on here. If you don't answer me back, I'll phone and disturb you hourly.

I'll try to distract you with murder theories. I know I'm going to throw too much at you at one time, but what else is new? You wanted my feedback, so here it is.

If Milt didn't do it (you're sure, right?), there are lots of other possibilities:

1. People who deliberately wanted to kill Marla Solomon:

Since the police found that incriminating evidence linking Milt to the crime, it's obvious they won't be bothering to search out Marla's enemies, right? You might have to start nosing them out when you're feeling better. Lotsa luck. Her family sounds devoted.

2. People who wanted to frame Milt for murder and didn't care who the victim was. Here you could have:

(a) One or more of the employees, most of whom don't sound too appetizing, you must admit;

(b) Someone from the outside whom you don't know about yet but who hates Milt.

3. Frankly, I think you now have a more important priority, kiddo. The reason you're feeling doomsdayish is because Stu was killed by a hit-and-run driver, and these recent events are obviously bringing the whole incident back to you in one emotional heap. So take care of yourself and *get to the doctor.*

chapter
7

....

Needless to say, Nan's e-mail gets my attention. We bat the out-to-get-me idea back and forth for the rest of the night and I end up doing double duty this morning— first seeing the doctor and then burying myself in my dusty attic to leaf through Stu's old file cabinets. Nan's not always right—it turns out I have no concussion, I'm just bruised and sore. I'm considering myself lucky and getting back to my other priorities.

Nan's final idea before we called it quits last night was that since Stu kept such detailed records I should see if he had any correspondence from Marla or notes that might give me a clue as to anything unusual going on in her life. Many congregants confide in their rabbi. Stu had people booked up constantly for counseling. He was one of those rabbis who really listened, and people responded by unloading their problems whenever they saw him. He didn't mind being dragged off into cor-ners—he said it energized him—that being close was more essential to what he stood for than preaching to the throngs, even though there was a place for that, too. I once heard him tell Turner, "Distance doesn't do it for me. The feedback from a big crowd's not what makes me tick."

But not everybody comes to a rabbi. Some are too concerned with keeping up appearances to expose any weaknesses or family secrets. Still others head for a therapist—not a clergyman. What little I know about Marla Solomon puts her in a fourth category—she'd probably be worried that Essie Sue would find out anything she told someone connected to the Temple. Of course, for all I know, Essie Sue could have known all Marla's secrets, assuming she had any.

Stu was so careful to keep confidences that he used to write very cryptic notes, and he never put them in the common files. Still, there's a chance I'll run across something not confidential that can help. I'm still not ready to see his handwriting and read his familiar expressions—one little phrase can rip right through the carefully created defenses I've built in the year and a half since his death. Just when I think I'm over the worst, the pain comes back. I comfort myself by leaning over to pat Oy Vay, who's curled up beside me.

Oy Vay's my three-legged golden retriever, so named because that's what Joshie's grandmother said when she heard we were getting a dog. We fell in love with a three-legged puppy whose leg had been crushed when her mother rolled over on it two days after her birth.

"Jews don't have dogs," Grandma informed us. "And a rabbi's household, to boot? What if he bites one of the congregants?"

We didn't tell her anything more about the dog, but when she saw her in person she could only say, "This *tsuris* you didn't need."

Oy Vay's almost as big as I am now, and I'm thankful for her every day. I give her stomach one more rub before tackling Stu's old files. There are four file cabinets I've saved from his old study—each stuffed full. I look through names and subjects. Nothing obvious about Marla.

Today is overcast and most of the attic is in deep shadow, making the faded file folders especially difficult to read. I'm sore and my head hurts. I'm on the third file cabinet and have one more to go through after that. I'm just about to take a break and lie down on the soft flowered sofa from our first apartment, from before Joshie was born, before our first congregation—a comforting, much-loved and loved-on reminder of old times—when I come across a ruled loose-leaf page, its three holes torn from a notebook. Stu's familiar script scrawls across the page. At first I don't see the tiny microcassette tape because Stu has apparently stuffed it between the S's and the T's in the third file cabinet. Its odd placement between folders makes me pay attention.

I'm uneasy. Since there's no comfort food around (where's a cuppa matzo ball soup when you need it?) I decide to flop on the sofa after all, as soon as I dig out Stu's old dictating recorder. Only two messages are on the tape:

January 28, 1 P.M.
Received a phone call this afternoon at temple that I suppose I should document. Had just come back

to my study from the graveside ceremony for Ron Bateman when they put the call through. The man had a low, raspy intonation and said, "Rabbi, this is a warning. Stay away from The Hot Bagel. You have no business there."

When I asked who this was and what did he mean, he said, "You heard me. If you go back, you'll be sorry."

Then he hung up. A meshuganah. Maybe a competitor trying to keep people away. Milt has ulcers about the place as it is. He doesn't need this to worry about. Hope this is the last of it.

February 13, 7 P.M.

Got another call before the board meeting tonight from the meshuganah.

He said, "Rabbi, you didn't take my advice. I'm warning you once more—if you don't stay away from The Hot Bagel, something bad is going to happen to you."

I said, "Who are you? If you don't tell me what this is about right now, I'm going to Milt Aboud and the police first thing in the morning."

Luckily, I'm lying on the sofa. I'm sure my legs would have buckled under me otherwise. Stu had never mentioned anything about the first call. This isn't surprising since he wouldn't have wanted to worry me—at least not with the first call. He dealt with such a big slice of humanity that the occasional odd phone call was almost common-place, and he never automatically assumed the worst about people.

But the second call? That was different. He was obviously concerned enough to change his mind and decide to tell Milt and the police.

To say I'm in shock would be an understatement. The implications of this are almost paralyzing. As I lie here in my attic in the gathering darkness of this rainy afternoon, it hits me that Stu's accident by hit-and-run wasn't an accident at all. As he left the Temple for home at nine o'clock that night, probably ready to tell me about the call before going to the police the next day, the killer made sure he never told anyone. He was waiting as Stu crossed the side street to the parking lot.

I know I'm not jumping to conclusions. The second threatening call, the truly ominous one, was made on February 13—the night Stu died.

chapter

8

....

E-mail from: Nan
To: Ruby
Subject: *Speechless*

I'm totally blown away by this news, and I'm fear-
ing for your sanity, babe. If all these revelations were
coming at *me*, I'd be on the shrink's couch. Meanwhile, feel free to use me as a sounding board. As if
you don't already!

You asked where you should go from here, and as
usual, answered your own question in the same e-mail.
But I did like most your idea about first talking to Milt,
now that he's out on bail. The heart of this current puzzle
is that there was something going on at the bakery, or
something going on or about to go on between Milt and
Stu—that the guy who threatened Stu wanted to stop.
You need to find out what Milt and Stu talked about or
had in common. I realize that Milt might not be so in-

terested in this, but maybe he'll be glad to think about something other than Marla.

I'm glad you finally became frightened enough after finding Stu's tape to go to the police, and I'm sorry they were so leery of reopening the investigation into Stu's death on the basis of, how did you put it, "two crank calls from a nut."

Look, I've held back for a whole e-mail on what's uppermost in my mind right now, so I'm just going to come out with it. Now that Stu's hit-and-run is suspicious, *maybe someone was trying to hit you, too.* Think about it.

What do you think this Lieutenant Lundy you spoke to is going to do with the police report of your own accident? Since he's a good customer in the bakery, maybe he'll take a personal interest. At any rate, now that you've talked to the police, it should be easier to say anything you want to Milt without feeling you're holding back from the officials.

By the way, are you doing anything for fun? Don't blow this off, Ruby. I think you should do something to relieve the stress.

....

E-mail from: Ruby
To: Nan
Subject: *Stress, Fries, and Audiotape*

Relieve the stress? Ha! I'm back to twisting my hair, and I haven't done that since seventh grade. And I write to *you* to relieve my stress. Since I can't worry twenty-four hours a day about being run down by a car, I'm dividing my time between french fries from Texas Tater—an old addiction I resurrected this week, and Southern Comfort.

Just kidding about the Southern Comfort. One addiction at a time is all I can handle.

I have a meeting with Milt tomorrow morning, which I intend to report to Lieutenant Lundy informally if anything comes from it. I'm going to tape the conversation with Milt so I can fine-comb it later.

Oh yeah—one stress-reliever did pop up, and since we can both use a break from the gloom around here, I'll tell you about it. The Rabbinical Selection Committee made its choice. Surprise, surprise—Essie Sue got her way and Charismatic Rabbi Kevin Kapstein will be gracing our fair pulpit. Maybe he'll be okay—I'm just glad the whole process is over. Having someone new here will help all of us move on. Since he insists on being called Rabbi Kapstein by one and all, I'll be calling him Rabbi Kevin to you.

This is the kicker, though. Remember the Stepford Wife, Jewish Version? The one who spectacularized Rabbi Kevin ad nauseam, went through the buffet line for him at every bar mitzvah lunch, and swooned during his sermons? My private name for her was Mrs. Stepstein. Anyway, to Essie Sue's grievous disappointment, Mrs. Stepstein will not be spending the rest of her life with us.

After Rabbi Kevin officially signed the contract, Essie Sue personally received the following letter from the rabbi (yo—he got the message real fast as to who runs the place, yes?) and had the message copied for the entire board:

My Dear Mrs. Margolis,

I want to thank you personally for your hospitality during my stay in my future home of Eternal, Texas, and for giving me that extra-special six-hour guided tour of Temple Rita. The lunch break, complete with boxed lunch made with your own hands, was something I shall never forget. The unusual champagne and herring Jell-O mold in the shape of Ellis Island was surpassed only by the iced coffee cubes in the form of the State of Texas which graced the latte. I have never enjoyed a more elegant repast.

I regret to inform you that I will be assuming my position alone—my wife Kitselah will not be joining me. Kitselah has run away with the proprietor of Manuel's Massage World: Different Strokes for Different Folks. *She left a note saying only that she could use the strokes.*

It pains me to say that Manuel is not Jewish.

As you can imagine, I am crushed over this turn of events, and had no inkling of these problems when I met with all of you in Eternal last week. My wife and I had the perfect "whither thou goest, I shall go" marriage, balanced in every way—wherever I went, she went. She anticipated my every need.

Kitselah is changing her name to Sojourner.

As I draw this letter to a close, dear Essie Sue, grieve with me for the end of a wonderful partnership but also a new beginning.

Faithfully,
Rabbi Kapstein

P.S. It goes without saying that you have my full support in your fabulous plan to erect a life-sized statue of Queen Esther in the likeness of your beloved sister.

....

E-mail from: Nan
To: Ruby
Subject: *Just a Thought.*

What do you think the odds are that the rabbi kept this little family secret about the runaway wife until *after* he signed the contract for the new job?

chapter

9

....

Milt looks as if he'd lost ten pounds.

"Only five," he says. "Any other time, I'd be thrilled."

Telling him to take the loss where he finds it, I head for the coffee machine and help myself to my first cup of the morning. It's an hour before opening time, and wonderful wafts of pumpernickel and rye are drifting my way. I pour us both a steaming cup of the real stuff, caffeinated and black. This morning it's Kenya roast. I eat the first sample from the ovens. Milt eats nothing. He looks fit now that he's a little thinner, with only the enormous dark circles under his eyes to betray the perfect picture. He's been coming in at odd hours to supervise, but doing a disappearing act around mealtimes, letting Grace, or the older help, or occasionally me oversee the place.

This seems sensible to me. As Milt says, "People are bound to feel uncomfortable being around the guy who's supposed to have murdered one of his customers."

"I'm worried about *you*," he says. "Are you having any aftershocks from the near miss the other night?"

"No, I'm recovered," I lie. I decide for several reasons to plunge into the subject that's on my mind. First, Milt doesn't need to dwell on my problems. Second, I don't think I can be of any help right now as to the question of who poisoned Marla. The police interviewed the women whose table Marla had stopped by when she bit into the poisoned bagel. Nobody at the table seemed to have a clue, according to Milt's attorney, Turner. Marla's family had been no gold mine of information, either—there's just the daughter, Glenda, Essie Sue and Hal Margolis, and some cousins. There just aren't any obvious villains in the group, and Milt's fingerprints on the poisoned vial give him both means and opportunity. His motive's weak, but what else is new?

"I passed Essie Sue on the street the other day and she looked at me as if I were roadkill," Milt says. "This is pure nightmare."

"Putting aside her longtime grudge against you," I say, "what else can she assume but what the police tell her? I'm not taking up for her—she's nuts to hold on to her resentment against you for all these years, but they've practically stopped investigating anyone else since they found the fingerprints. Do you think Essie Sue wanted Marla dead for some reason and decided to frame you?" I'm being a bit paranoid, but I throw that out to him.

"No. Maybe. I don't know. Who am I, Sherlock Holmes?"

"Sorry." I'm beginning to think I'm the last person who should be talking to Milt right now—I'm feeling pretty insane with all these thoughts whirling around in what passes for my brain. I revert back to my original notion of asking very specific questions about those threatening calls to Stu.

"Milt, do you have any idea why someone would have wanted Stu to stay away from your bakery?"

"I've racked my brain and I can't think of anything."

"Maybe we can brainstorm about what brought you two together in the first place. All I remember is he hung out here a lot in the early years, and later we both loved the place. And loved you."

"Thanks, hon. Grace and I feel the same way."

"Did you ever confide in one another about problems?"

"We talked about our families a lot, but no confidences worth threatening phone calls from nutcases, if that's what you mean."

"You mean family stuff like Grace and me?"

"No. I mean our childhood families—the New York connection. Even though we didn't know each other as kids, Stu's uncles up there knew my father better than I did. If you remember my telling you, my parents were divorced when I was three, and my mother and I moved away from New York right after. By the time she married my stepdad, all the New York relatives had become like a blur to me but I heard stories secondhand. Talking to Stu made the New York memories seem more real. Do you still keep up with Stu's relatives?"

"Sure. They're very prolific. I get bar mitzvah invitations all the time, but I don't really know the kids. I'm fond of the older generation, though. An invitation came a couple of weeks ago and I was considering it—before all hell broke loose around here. Uncle Aaron's having an eightieth birthday next month, and he wants me to come up. Stu loved his uncles. They were very kind when Stu died, and are always telling me they want me to stay close to his family."

"You ought to go."

"This is not a good time. I have all kinds of plans lined up. The new rabbi's coming to town next week, and Essie Sue made a deal with me. If I come to one of the dinner parties she's throwing to welcome him, she'll make some time for me to ask her questions about Marla. She's agreed to brainstorm with me about her sister's life and times. I can't think of a worse time for me to be away."

"I can't think of a better one. I'd feel a lot happier if you were out of the way of any stray vehicles that might run you down, and my case is dragging on at this point so I don't think there's much you can do for me. Now that school's starting and she doesn't have to keep the kids, Grace can spend more time here in the shop, so you don't have to worry on that score. Why can't you go to Essie Sue's party and then leave for New York?"

I avoid an answer. "What I wish I could do is find a clue as to Marla's killer instead of being deluged with paranoia over my own hit-and-run and the threats to Stu. Marla's death seems so senseless at this point—as if it were unconnected to anything real. I'd like to be spending my time following up clues to *her* murder."

"Look, Ruby, Turner and I can't think of anyone who'd kill Marla, either. Keep digging into the hit-and-runs—your life could be on the line."

The counter help drift in to get ready for the lunchtime

trade. Carol Sealy does seem to have a crush on Milt, though it's harmless enough. She has a way of touching his arm as she goes by him.

"Hey, Milt," she says. "You better not let your girl-friend play manager too much. She has lots of ideas about changing things. Your wife wouldn't like it."

We ignore the girlfriend bit.

"Oh, I know all about Ruby's changes, Carol. She's been trying to automate this place for years. Ruby'd have me faxing bagels if she had her way."

"Did you know she'd like to have a reading section?"

"Yeah, tattletale. I know all about the *Atlantic Monthly* casually tossed next to the toasted sesame. Don't take it too seriously." He grins at me, and I'm happy to see him smile. I would have fumed a couple of months ago about the little twit and her remarks. Now I couldn't care less. Funny how quickly a few horrors in your life can teach you not to sweat the small things.

I have a sudden urge to see my one and only all-grown-up baby Joshie, who has two weeks off between his job as head counselor at a summer camp and the fall semester of college. I guess it's good we can't see into the future. I'd never have dreamed his undergraduate years would have been so bittersweet. Having your dad taken away so abruptly and completely forever changes your experience of the carefree campus life. Josh wanted to drop out for a semester after Stu died, but I talked him out of it. It wouldn't have helped either of us. He came home for lots of weekends and cheered me im-measurably, but he was nineteen, and I wanted him to return quickly to his world.

I wonder if Joshie would want to go to this family

weekend in New York with me. I'd like him to know his dad's relatives and to have them know him. It would be great to take a trip together.

Grace is just coming in to take over the lunch hour. I reach over and give Milt a big hug. Grace looks as haggard as he does. She's a beautiful brunette, but her energy sags inward these days. This experience has put ten years on her. We hug, too, and don't need to say much to each other.

As I go out the door, Milt hands me a bag of fresh bagels and says, "Do me a favor and think about that trip."

Maybe I will and maybe I won't. Right now, I'm headed back to my attic to finish checking out the last file cabinet.

chapter
10

···················

E-mail from: Ruby
To: Nan
Subject: More Tales from the Crypt

I'm feeling positively ghoulish these days holed up in my gloomy attic, resurrecting old notes Stu didn't even want me to see. I'm convinced, though, that the key to all this lies somewhere in his files. I did find something today that clarified the connection between Milt's family and Stu's. I was looking up letters from Stu's family and came across an old one from his uncle Aaron, the relative closest to Stu after his mother and father died. Aaron was married to Stu's mother's sister, and was always crazy about his sister-in-law's kids.

Aaron's great. He's bald-headed and innocent-looking, but that round head holds more brains than a trainload of Mensas, with a wicked sense of humor that won't quit. He's the one who's celebrating his eightieth birthday next month.

Aaron's letter was dated twenty years ago. Stu had obviously written to Aaron about his new friendship with Milt Aboud. Aaron wrote back that he had gone to work in his father's bakery in Brooklyn in 1933 as a young man. To make bagels in New York in the thirties, you had to be a member of Bagel Bakers Local 338, a union of only three hundred workers. Admission was to sons of members only. This was why there was always a shortage of good bagels in the city, and why people had to line up early in the morning to buy a fresh bag of hot bagels before the bakery ran out.

Aaron remembered Milt's family. All he said about them was "one time they got in big trouble with the union and they were ready to kill each other over it."

I'd love to know more about this, Nan. Uncle Aaron hates the telephone. He claims it drove him crazy when he was in business. All he'll say on the phone is "Yes," "No," and "Wrong number," and I didn't get much from the letter, so my best bet is probably to get the information out of him in person. I checked with Milt and he said there was some big family scandal his mother only hinted at. Although she and his father had no contact at all, she told Milt she wouldn't bad-mouth his father to him in the hope he might get an inheritance some day. In fact, he did get a small inheritance from his real dad and he used it to start The Hot Bagel. But he didn't know a lot about the business until he opened the franchise. He learned from the training seminars given by the people who sold him a bagel machine—the modern invention that does what the bakers used to do by hand—roll and shape the bagels.

Maybe Aaron was being facetious when he said Milt's

family was ready to kill one another, but just hearing that word makes me want to investigate.

The problem is I don't want to travel right now—but you already know that.

....

E-mail from: Nan
To: Ruby
Subject: What Are You Waiting For?

1. The airlines are having a fare war and you can make the twenty-one-day limit if you hurry.

2. Take Joshie before classes start.

3. Surely you're not going to gamble that an eighty-year-old man will be around forever?

4. Go!

....

E-mail from: Ruby
To: Nan
Subject: Leaving in Two Weeks—After Labor Day

You talked me into it!

chapter
11

....

Well, this is the big night. Walking into Essie Sue's living room is like entering Never-Never Land. Two white couches at right angles enclose a pristine space containing a long glass-and-stainless-steel cocktail table. The two-year-old copy of *Architectural Digest* must have been set on the glass tabletop with a compass—it lies perfectly straight at one corner, and woe to her who nudges it out of line. I always keep my distance from that *Architectural Digest*. Tonight there's a copy of *Texas Monthly* set squarely on top of the *Digest*, and on top of that is Leo Rosten's ancient best-seller, *The Joys of Yiddish*, in the rabbi's honor. A silver tray holds square cocktail rye slices precisely dominoed toward the cream cheese block. I always bet on which guest will be hungry enough to actually disturb the rye slices and get cream cheese all over the polished serving knife.

My bet is on Brother Copeland, in sport shirt and slacks, who's here with his wife Yvonne. His brother

Buster is not invited—Essie Sue doesn't like him. Thank goodness Yvonne's here. I've always enjoyed her— she's smart and fun to kibbitz with. I expected a bigger crowd for this party. So far, the only other person I see is the host, Essie Sue's dour husband Hal Margolis, who's over in the corner trying to pour himself a bourbon and branch water. Trying is the apt expression.

"Sugar," Essie calls, "please give the help a chance to wait on you after they bring in the glasses from the kitchen. A little patience is all I ask." She's always called him Sugar, despite the fact that the man has a countenance so dismal he makes Boris Karloff look like a barrel of laughs. I've always empathized with him.

Hal seems quite anxious to pour that bourbon. He raises an empty glass toward Brother for encouragement, but Brother's looking the other way toward the cream cheese, about to make his move.

"So where's the guest of honor?" I ask Essie Sue. The rabbi is staying with the Margolises until he finds a place to live.

"Soon, dear. He napped this afternoon, and now he's dressing." She smiles sweetly at me. I wonder why. I instinctively pat myself down, waiting for a studied remark about my appearance, or recent activities, or whatever. I've made sure to wear a black top tonight, just in case. There's something about Essie Sue's dinner parties that deregulates my spill-control mechanism. Now, when the inevitable falls on my chest at the dinner table, it won't show. Who am I kidding—she'll see it anyway.

Essie Sue turns toward the hall door and clinks on a glass.

"Ladies and gentlemen, I hear our guest of honor. Let me introduce Rabbi Kevin Kapstein."

Rabbi Kapstein, beaming, makes his entrance and heads over to hug his hostess. He's short, dressed in a dark suit, white shirt, and tie—immaculate from the waist up, but his lower half doesn't quite match the top. Because he has no waistline, his trousers sag a bit over his wing tips. He looks his age—late thirties, they said, with the light brown hair Essie Sue described, but I'd describe it a bit differently—oddly cut and left long in back to cover a bald spot. Perfectly fine if you're not expecting spectacular. Spectacular he's not. I try to concentrate and not think of Mrs. Stepstein. But, of course, ever since my school days, many of which were spent on the principal's waiting room bench, I'm at my worst when I try *not* to think of something. I look over at Yvonne, but she, wisely for both of us, looks at the ceiling fan.

Essie Sue seems pleased. I'm happy for the woman. She's gone through plenty this year and I'm glad she likes the rabbi. I just hope it lasts. Something about the man tells me he'll make sure it does. She hugs him and leads him to each of us in turn. When she gets to me, she says, "This is the woman I told you about, Rabbi." I'm wondering exactly what she told him, but I gamely stay in the •here and now. I put out my hand and he scoops it up with both of his. They're damp. That's okay, I tell myself. I'd be nervous, too, in this company. The voice from my principal's office days tells me, "Funny, but he doesn't *look* nervous. Maybe he just has damp hands."

Later, much later, I'll find myself thinking I would

have liked him more if he *had* been nervous. But for now, I play the greeting game with the best of them. After we all smile many times, Essie Sue calls us to dinner. The "help" has arrived in force. Essie Sue's regular day cleaner is not company material. In fact, it's a bit hard for her to keep day help. But at any rate, for parties she hires her help from Ben's Party Parlour. Ben's help consists mostly of young men from the university athletic department who play sports other than the more popular football or basketball. They're not the most efficient help, but Ben always sees that they wear tuxedos. Essie Sue is very good at summoning the help with a bell. As far as I know, she's the only person in Eternal who uses a bell, but she uses it very well.

My black place card tells me in gold letters where I'm seated—next to the rabbi. There are only six of us, but Essie Sue would do without the entree before she'd do without place cards. The centerpiece appears to be something rabbinical. Don't ask. On the menu is poached salmon, which I love, and among other things, grits. We're told this is the hostess's way of introducing the rabbi to Texas cooking. I let this pass. I'm on my best behavior tonight, and I aim to make good conversation.

The rabbi looks as though he'd be easy to talk to, and I'm an expert at that, having been dragged kicking and screaming into the world of cocktail party talk years ago. I will very definitely avoid all mention of the runaway wife. Boy, would I like to know about *that*. But I can't. So I won't.

He says, "Ruby, I've heard so much about you from Essie Sue."

"Thanks, Kevin," I say, "I hope some of it was good."

Not scintillating, but I'm not inspired yet. And besides, I'm having to avoid all the good stuff.

Kevin looks perturbed, and I know it's nothing I've said, since so far the conversation's been Small Talk 101.

Essie Sue can't hear us, but I can tell she doesn't like the look on his face. She gives me a warning glance, but at least it's not the nasty warning snarl she's favored me with in the past. I ignore it but I do keep my voice down.

"Is something bothering you?" I ask.

"You called me Kevin. I'm Rabbi Kapstein."

Now it all comes back to me.

"You did call me Ruby, didn't you? Wasn't that a hint that you preferred a first-name basis?"

He's going to be indulgent. "You're too pretty to be called Mrs. Rothman—that's for old ladies."

I know this isn't the right moment to pursue this, but I can't help myself.

"What happens when you're at professional meetings? Do your colleagues and their spouses get to call you Kevin? People who lived in the dorm with you at the seminary?" Everyone's listening by now.

"Still Rabbi Kapstein. It's a matter of honor."

I grit my grits.

"Then I'd prefer to be called Ms. Rothman. It's a matter of honor."

"Still too pretty," he says. To my horror he puts his arm around me.

Yvonne smiles sweetly and says, "Er . . . Rabbi, did your lil' ol' wife have to call you Rabbi Kapstein, too, in those wifely moments?"

The dinner table becomes totally still at this point—we're all agog. At least four of the six are agog. Essie Sue has jumped up to rescue her party from premature ruin.

"We'll adjourn to the living room for kiwi tarts and espresso. I know we all have so much to ask the rabbi."

Gag me with a demitasse spoon.

I sit at the end of the sofa and frantically eyeball Yvonne to sit beside me, but the rabbi has recovered and beats her to it. This guy's a brick wall. And why is he chasing me around?

All my rabbinical social evenings are coming back to me, and it's not a pretty sight. I'm so thankful Stu was a normal man and not an egomaniac—if his personality had been even the slightest bit heavy on the narcissistic side, he would have taken to these gatherings like a pig wallowing in grease, if you'll pardon the expression. Instead, he fought them like crazy.

We now begin to play what I call Ring-Around-the-Rabbi. I'm not talking classroom here, where this might be expected behavior, but just any social gathering. Put a rabbi in the room and all normal conversation ceases. The entire evening becomes a question-and-answer session, with the rabbi giving the answers. The room can be full of brilliant minds who, in other settings, can argue, discuss, laugh, cry, and ignite one another. Suddenly, they all become neophytes, their questions on early Sunday School level or worse. People don't seem to realize this is happening, and the rabbi can either buy in to it or not.

Kevin buys. At first, I give him the benefit of the doubt, since we don't know him and he *is* the guest of honor. But every time the conversation turns away from him, he leans his head back and "rests" his eyes. He never, ever, asks a question of someone else, but he wakes up real fast whenever the talk turns back to him. After a while we *all* drift off—except for Essie Sue, who's loving it.

I find myself counting calendar years instead of sheep. It's gonna be a long tenure.

Yvonne and I try to escape to the powder room at the same time, but Essie Sue catches us and makes me wait in line until after Yvonne's turn. When I come back, I sit in a different place, but Kevin follows. I've only stayed this long because Essie Sue promised to talk to me about Marla, and I'm determined to collect. During a moment when I'm hoping even she's had her fill of the question-and-answer session, I pull her aside.

"How about now?" I ask, knowing she's going to put me off until the end of the evening. To my surprise, she says we can talk for a few minutes in her bedroom suite, aka Mauve World. Mauve rules the day here, with matching tasteful prints in everything from the bed ruffle to the pencil holder on the end table to the Kleenex box in the bathroom. Nothing has been missed—even the closet is lined in mauve print. I don't want to say too much about her shoe collection housed in mauve print shoe cases, but Imelda Marcos would feel right at home. Hal's presence is nowhere to be seen or felt, of course. There's not much question as to who's Master of the Master Suite.

We girls curl up on the bed, with me still in shock that she's being so nice to me. Not that she's much help with my inquiries, since she already knows who done it.

I ask her to imagine there's no Milt in the picture.

"Is there anyone in the family who had a grudge against Marla?"

"No one," she says. I believe her. We go through a rundown of the three women whose table Marla and Essie Sue stopped by on their way out of the bakery. Even though I knew a couple of them, I want to hear what Essie Sue has to say. One of them, I point out, could have offered her the bagel that killed her.

"No," Essie Sue says. "I specifically remember Marla taking the top bagel out of her own bag and taking a bite of it. I'll never forget it."

"One of the women could have slipped the bagel on top when no one was looking," I say. "Marla liked these women?"

"Annie Ratner has known Marla all her life. They used to live down the street from us. She and Marla cut out paper dolls together."

Now, *that's* a motive. The problem is that as far as I can tell, Marla Solomon was beige on beige. I just can't find any drama connected to her at all. She had some life insurance made out to her daughter. So what? Glenda has a good job as a bank manager, owns her own home, and I don't think Las Vegas is after her. I dutifully ask about the other women.

"Bela Brown is the grandmother of three and sells fancy combs at craft shows. She's a comb collector. Fran Jergens is the office manager for the company that handles the ads for the yellow pages. Annie Ratner is the only one who could be called a friend—the others, she just knew."

Essie Sue gets off the bed—my signal the questioning

period is over. "Now we don't have to be bothered with this later," she says. "And by the way, what do you think of the new rabbi?"

I'm speechless. My mind's been on Marla, but I should have been ready for this.

Essie Sue doesn't push.

"You'll have lots of time to know him," she says benignly.

I'm thinking that's the problem.

We rejoin the others and it's as if we were never gone—he's holding court and they're mute. The clock keeps ticking as Rabbi Kapstein broadcasts his many opinions:

On Jewish teenagers' dating habits: "Guilt, guilt, guilt! If you make 'em feel guilty enough, they'll only go out with Jews."

The elect versus the nonelect: "Attendance, attendance, attendance! The ones who attend services every week are the *real* Jews, and everybody knows it."

It's getting late and finally we all sense that we're about to be sprung from the dinner party from hell, but not before a little boost from Essie Sue.

"See what I told you? This man has charisma if I ever heard charisma." We nod glazed-eyed, ready to agree to anything.

Essie Sue draws me aside and says in a voice that could melt butter, "Ruby, honey, Rabbi Kapstein has asked me if he can escort you home." Rabbi Kapstein gives me a little wave behind her back.

"But I rode over with Brother and Yvonne."

"I'm sure they won't mind giving way to this."

This? What's *this*? Being escorted home is the last thing I need. "Maybe some other time, Essie Sue. It's late tonight." I find myself in sudden need of the after-dinner brandy Hal has been pushing vainly on me all evening. I back up toward the bar to get out of Essie Sue's direct line of fire.

I gesture for a small one and he pours. Hal's a man of no words, but we understand each other.

"Quite a night," I say, "and I'm getting some awfully strange vibes."

"Better believe it," he says. "She's got a new job description in mind for you."

I'm sure it's the bourbon talking.

chapter
12

....

I see Joshie's red mop of hair moving above the tired mob headed down the ramp of Gate 31 at DFW. I used to love cutting that hair myself when he was a baby—it was straight, thick, and just made for running your fingers through. The hair's darkened maybe one shade since then, but it still flames over everything in sight. Tall, thin, and wiry like his dad, Joshie's hard to miss in a crowd.

"Hey, Mom!" His hug's a bear hug—his long arms and legs, perfectly suited for the rock climbing and kayaking he loves to do, are stronger than their slender circumference would suggest. He's wearing chinos.

"Very fifties," I say when I can get my breath. I try very hard not to do a mother trip on him in public, but the truth is I just want to gaze at him for a while.

"Yeah, some of the pants from your time feel real comfortable."

I remind him that the fifties was only the decade of

my birth, not really my time. "But who knows? Maybe I had khaki baby clothes."

"How was your flight?" we both ask each other in the same breath. This is a phenomenon we're used to. Sometimes I think our minds were genetically hardwired. "Fine," we say, without batting an eyelash. We've both flown separately to Dallas so we can go on to New York together. Getting away right now is the best gift I can give myself, and having Joshie come with me makes it special.

As we march down yet another aisle and settle ourselves on the flight to La Guardia, I try to figure out how I'm going to tell him all that's happened in the last few weeks. He knows about Marla's murder, but I've told him nothing about the events surrounding the hit-and-runs.

I chicken out almost immediately. It feels too good just to relax and schmooze—I'll worry about the rest later. I want to hear about his summer job, but he wants to talk about the trip.

"So let's talk about New York. Who are all these relatives? I wasn't too with it at Dad's funeral. I just remember Dad always loved Uncle Aaron."

"Most of these relatives didn't come to the funeral—they never ventured out of New York when they were younger, much less now when travel's so hard for them. Aaron and Becky were the ones we were close to. I think you'll get a kick out of staying in their apartment on the West Side. Nothing's changed there for the last fifty years."

"Where is it?" He's spread out a big map of New

York—a passion he inherited from me. If I can't see it on a map, I don't believe I'm there.

"Riverside in the low Nineties—not too far from Columbia. Their apartment's three bedrooms, rent-controlled, and not gentrified yet. You'll love nosing in the bookstores and little restaurants around there. Every day for fifty years Aaron took the subway—the IRT local to Columbus Circle, changed for the D train, changed again at Rockefeller Center for the F—all the way to the Lower East Side to his bakery. Living closer would have been a lot easier, but they like it where they are. I once asked him and he said, 'Work is work and life is life with a subway ride in between.' "

"A man who knows his own mind. I'd like living a life that's just the opposite, you know? I want my work and my life to be mixed, and whatever it is, it has to be outside."

No surprises here. Josh was seduced by the out-of-doors almost from the beginning, when Stu took him canoeing in an infant life jacket and hiking from a back-pack seat. The two of them spent time alone doing more rugged camping as Joshie grew into it, and he learned to love it.

Now that I'm more relaxed and the trip's half over, I realize I need to take this quiet time to bring him up to date on what's really been going on. It's as good a time as any, and if I'm going to be doing some real digging on this trip, he can be helpful, too. He listens intently, not interrupting until I'm finished.

"I'm scared for you, Mom. I think it's nuts for you to go to New York to explore some connection between Dad and Milt. Okay, not nuts exactly, but why aren't you finding out more about your own hit-and-run?"

"Because I didn't see the car, I could give the police no clues—basically, I have nothing. I don't even know if the near miss was deliberate or an accident. I received no threats like your dad did, and as far as I know, there's no one who would want to kill me."

"So we're stuck?" His shift to "we" is just like him.

"Yeah. We're stuck, honey. And you forget—this isn't just a fishing expedition. I needed to get away, and it makes me happy to see Uncle Aaron for his big birthday. If I learn something in the bargain, then it's all for the better. And you know how I feel about following my hunches."

The cab from La Guardia makes good time across the Triborough, and we segue across Manhattan at 110th, past the Cathedral of St. John the Divine, then across Broadway, West End, to Riverside Drive. I'm just thinking how amazing it is that the weather is clear enough to see the barges on the river when it begins to rain. *Now* we're in New York.

"You really get off on this place, don't you, Mom? Now that you're on your own, do you ever think of living here?"

"No, I won't live here. But I do love it."

"Like I love the mountains?"

Wow. He gets it—in a way none of my friends get it.

"Exactly the way you love the mountains. This place is a natural wonder. I don't have to be here to know it's here. Just like you're not going to spend all your time on a mountaintop, I don't have to live here to have it energize me. You know how some people feel more 'Jewish' in Israel than they do at home? They're there five minutes and they feel they belong? That's what New York does to me."

"You always did gravitate to New Yorkers—even at home. Remember the guy who owned that 'TV Repair on Wheels' truck who ended up spending all afternoon at the house drinking your Zabar's coffee and talking about restaurants in Little Italy?"

"I can't believe you remember that. He still fixes my TV, and he's a good example of what I meant. Sal's not even Jewish. There's a whole New York flavor that's not specifically Jewish, but if you took the Jewish essence out of it, it wouldn't be as New York-ey."

"So which came first, the chicken or the egg?"

"They blend, like good chopped liver with boiled eggs and chicken schmaltz."

"You know what I liked about the TV guy? Aside from the fact that he let me use his wrench case on my bicycle? He wasn't all one thing or all the other, like a lot of the Bubbas I know. He knew TVs, but he also had an opinion on borough politics and why the mafia bosses improved the garbage collections and which music store would give you the most money for old Caruso records."

"If you appreciated Sal, you're going to love Uncle Aaron, Joshie. His jokes have that cerebral edge and he's a very up-front guy."

"Even at eighty?"

"Especially at eighty. As he says, 'In your eighties, all the masks are down.' "

Our cab pulls up to the redbricked apartment building and we fight to get out the door before two couples waiting in the rain push through us in a race for the backseat. In a sure sign that the city has already enveloped us, we don't bother looking back to see who wins.

chapter
13

....

The birthday party for Uncle Aaron gives every ap-
pearance of being a big success. Joshie is surrounded by
enough cousins and cousins-in-law to fill half the state
of New Jersey, and every inch of space in the huge high-
ceilinged dining room is taken up either by food or those
eating it. Everyone's eating and talking and interrupting
at the same time. In other words, the usual. The massive
oak dining room table is much too sturdy to groan under
the weight of anything, but tonight it's challenged. An
eightieth birthday is significant—maybe a convenient
paper plate would have been perfect for transporting
schnecken for an afternoon visit, but tonight every relative has hauled out sterling silver with curlicued feet to
hold the fresh-baked mandelbrot, lemon bundt cake, and
aromatic rugelach. Most of the feast is homemade, and
what isn't is still special, like the giant strawberry
cheesecake from Greenberg's, brought by some of the
yuppier cousins. If Dr. Atkins could ignore the carbo-

hydrates and Dean Ornish would forget the fats, they'd both be happy here. Heart healthy it's not, but as I look around it occurs to me that it's very much about the heart. And since most of these octogenarians have been consuming this stuff for a lifetime, it does make you wonder.

Aside from the main guest of honor, we're considered minor celebrities, too, for having traveled so far. I'm happy to be part of this particular crowd, but I still have to fight my basic temperament, which is definitely tailored to one on one. Crowds overstimulate me. As traits go, that one was a real winner for a rabbi's wife, but that's another story. Tonight, though, I can handle it because I have a mission. I'm busy looking for people who might have been part of the bagel business in the old days.

I'm standing at the table munching one of the crispiest pieces of mandelbrot I've ever tasted when my eyes wander above the sideboard to a row of old photos on the dining room wall. Flanked by gilded sconces, no less. One of the photos is to die for—a group shot in that burnished gold sepia tone I've always loved. Four young men, in their late teens or barely out of them, are leaning together with their arms draped around one another. They wear tweed caps in various angles of rakishness, with knickers and thick kneesocks. One, on the end, looks so much like my nephew Nathan that I know it's his grandfather, Aaron. He's grinning. Next to him another family face looks out at me that has to be Aaron's brother Ben. The sophisticated one. He's trying to look nonchalant but not quite bringing it off—especially since his arms and feet are dusted with a white powder—flour, I'm sure. The remaining pair also belong together—they're brothers or maybe cousins.

These two are chunkier than Aaron or Ben, and both are very solemn. One has heavy eyebrows and looks like a professional worrier, and the other is pale, dreamy, and distant. I don't know the faces but there's a whiff of resemblance that I'm picking up from somewhere.

The boys are standing in front of a crooked sign that reads BAGEL BAKERS UNION LOCAL 338. I'm so engrossed in the photo I don't even notice Aaron coming up beside me.

"The Fearless Four," he says. "Me, my brother Ben, and our buddies Carl and Irv. They were brothers, too. We were all in the union together."

"When was this taken?"

Aaron took a closer look. "I'd say around '33. We all look pretty young. Nathan has more pictures down at the bakery. He took them out of his grandmother's scrapbook and framed them. For decor, he says, but I know he's attached to them. Funny how tradition skips a generation, isn't it? I could never get Maurie interested in the bakery at all, and now his own son wants to carry on the tradition."

"Does Nathan belong to the union, too?"

"Nah—the union's long gone, Ruby. When the bagel machines were invented, it broke the union. All the kneading and kettling and baking used to be done by hand—we learned it from our fathers and it made us a good living. But bad things could happen to you if you made bagels without the union backing."

"Bad things?"

"You don't know the half of it, honey. I'll take you around one day while you're here."

"They're looking for you, Uncle Aaron." Joshie comes over and motions me to come with him. I watch Aaron disappear into a knot of his cronies and I follow Josh out to the sooty terrace.

"Mom, I've been sleuthing for you. Guess who knows all the stories about the old days?"

Aaron's grandson Nathan is waiting for us outside. He's commandeered a plate of cheesecake and some black coffee.

"Hey," I say. "We can stay out here forever."

"All the necessities of living," Nathan assures me. "Cheesecake, coffee, and thou."

He's Aaron's grandson all right. I can see Joshie's happy. He's met a soul mate. Nathan looks like the Rothmans—tall and wiry with very dark hair straight as a board, and equally dark eyes.

"The eyes of a scholar," I say.

"You think so? I've always preferred working with my hands," he says, "but history grabs me—especially the kind you can reach out and touch, like Manhattan's old buildings."

Now he's really got me hooked. New York's architecture is a passion of mine—seldom indulged, but always with me. I've actually had cast-iron facades appear in my dreams. No wonder Joshie's excited.

"So tell her," he goads Nathan.

"Josh seemed to think you'd be interested in watching us make bagels. I've collected what's almost a little museum down on the Lower East Side in our front office.

Care to take a look? We still make 'em the old-fashioned way."

"And, Mom, he knows all kinds of stuff about the old local."

"I'm halfway there," I pant. "When can we come? Tomorrow?"

"Sure. Why don't I meet you after brunch at Ratner's on Delancey Street, and I'll walk you over to our place afterward. Things slow down in the afternoon and I can give you more time."

"Joshie doesn't know about Ratner's," I say.

"All I can tell you is, just don't eat breakfast," Nathan warns him.

chapter
14

·····················

The waiter at Ratner's almost wishes us a good day before remembering to revert to character. Instead, he bestows the large menus with a flourish worthy of Leonardo da Vinci's business manager offering the *Mona Lisa* up for auction. There's no doubt who's in charge here, and it's not the customer. Eating at Ratner's is a privilege, and you're not allowed to forget it despite the fact that you're the one paying. Remuneration here is merely homage to the divine. This is a dairy restaurant—corned beef will never kiss a cheese slice in this kitchen.

"The cherry cheese blintzes are not to be missed," our waiter demands, and both Joshie and I succumb in a nanosecond. Twenty minutes pass before they're ready, but the blintzes are served richly and dangerously sizling, with the sweet, aromatic cherry cheese mixture ozing from the folds of their pastry wrapping. With a cup of black coffee, this repast is as close to a taste of heaven as the city of New York can provide.

We float from the restaurant in a fog that matches the one outside, where a steady drizzle slicks the narrow streets. Umbrellas up and heads down, the noonday populace relentlessly feels its way through the rain, slowed down a bit except for the well-dressed matrons making a beeline for the handbag bargains at Fine and Klein. Nathan walks up just in time to guide us down the back-streets to the bagel bakery.

"If you're thinking of a cab, forget it," he says. "You won't find one, and if you did, the driver would kill you for only going six blocks. If we hurry along, we'll be there in no time."

We arrive slightly soaked, but the warmth of the ovens in the small space on Orchard Street relaxes muscles which had clenched unconsciously as we tried to fend off the rain. Balmy fragrances fill the air—not sweet, not pungent—just fresh and uncomplicated. The front room, which serves as the sales section, contains glassed-in counter units, now half-filled with shiny golden brown bagels. Photos, felt banners, statuettes, and memorabilia line the walls.

"I won't ask you if you want anything to eat," Nathan says. "When you shake yourselves off, though, you're welcome to look around at our collection." He points Joshie toward a small bronze statuette of a man on horseback.

"That's King John of Poland. He loved to ride. Isn't this a great replica? The original was made in the late seventeenth century, honoring the king for preventing the city of Vienna from being captured by the Turks."

He lifts up the statue. "See his foot in the riding stir-rup? A Viennese Jewish baker invented a hard roll with a hole in the middle, as a tribute to the king. The roll with the hole was supposed to represent a stirrup, so he called it *bugel*, the German word for stirrup."

"*Bugel* became *bagel*? Cool." Joshie's curiosity, like mine, keeps him going. I can see he's really into this.

While we're talking, a steady stream of customers files in and out, even though Nathan's cashier tells me this is the slow time of day. Milt would be green with envy—slow time in Eternal at The Hot Bagel means one or two customers. I want to look much more closely at the rest of the display, but Nathan's anxious to show us the ovens before the next big baking flurry in mid-afternoon.

"The morning rush is for people wanting bagels for breakfast," he says, "and for bags to take to the office. The big rush in the afternoon is to take home. My grandfather Aaron came here every weekday of his working life at four in the morning and stayed here until six at night."

This sounds like the restaurant business to me. I could never understand those people, either. There's a camaraderie among all these types, since they have to be workaholics to be successful. They eat, drink, and live the business. Yet somehow, Uncle Aaron managed to have a life apart from this.

The oven area in back is smaller than I had imagined. Only two workers are on duty—both of them stocky men, with huge muscular arms. After watching them bake for a while, I can understand how they develop those arms.

"All that's in the traditional bagel is yeast, malt, and flour," Nathan tells us. "This is Hugh and Eddie. They knead the bagel dough themselves—no machines—and shape the bagels by hand."

Hugh and Eddie raise floured hands in a hi. Eddie kneads, shapes the balls of dough, and pokes his thumb through to make the holes. After the bagels rise, Hugh drops them into a large kettle to boil.

"Boiling's the secret," Nathan says, "aside from the recipe for the blend of ingredients, which is also a secret. But the kettling is what makes the hard, shiny crust."

I watch, fascinated, as Hugh and Eddie place the boiled bagels on redwood boards covered with wet burlap. They lift a board into the oven and then flip it, turning the bagels over onto the oven shelf for baking.

"We can turn out about ten dozen bagels an hour," Hugh tells us. "We have two more guys in here during rush hours so we can double that."

I'm getting too hot, and anxious to go look at the photos, so I step outside, and the others follow. I head for the memorabilia.

A copy of the photo from Aaron's dining room is on a shelf along with several other sepia-toned enlargements. I notice that the Bagel Bakers Union sign is always in full view.

"What's with the union?" I ask Nathan. "Were they always hanging out there?"

"The union was like no other union at the time, Ruby. You have to remember that bagels had spread into cities all over Eastern Europe, and there was already a huge appetite for them built up when the immigrants came to New York. Many of the first shops were in the basements of tenements—then the better ones rented commercial space. Anyone controlling that market could be financially successful. The union exploited this by staying small and limiting membership only to sons of members. There were only about thirty or so shops in the whole New York area."

"Aaron got pulled away last night," I say, "before I could ask him about his buddies Carl and Irv and their union days. Any chance of pumping you instead?"

"I get a kick out of you, Ruby. You put it right out there, don't you? Carl and Irv were right at the heart of what happened." Nathan motions us over to one of only two small corner tables in the front room. Apparently, this bakery is for selling, not dining.

"You might as well know," he says, shrugging, "I'm a born yenta. I have an hour. Fire away. There's more gossip connected to the Bagel Bakers Union than there are crumbs in my ovens."

E-mail from: Ruby
To: Nan
Subject: Good News and Bad News

I told you I'd write once more while we were still in New York, since Nathan doesn't mind my using his computer at the bakery. This is it until I get home and give myself a few days to get settled, okay? I've got to catch up with work and see how Milt has survived.

I said good news and bad news. The bad news is that the stories Nathan peppered us with were mostly *bub-bemeisas*—old wives' tales with everything but the kitchen sink thrown in. There was a lot of bad blood in Milt's family, but Nathan's just heard bits and pieces of it. After all, he's only twenty-one years old.

The good news is that this kid is all the yenta we could have hoped for, and he's now primed to hone his curiosity and aim it toward finding specific answers for me. You know how I am when I get started. We found a long order form for his bakery supplies and I left him with a list of questions I wrote on the back of it. He didn't seem intimidated like most people who've been the recipients of my lists, so that's a good sign. Joshie just rolled his eyes, of course—but, Nan, I'm certain this is going to get results.

The most intriguing thing Nathan told us was that the dreamy one of the two brothers in that sepia photo I wrote you about turns out to be Milt's father! Remember he looked vaguely familiar to me? Milt's dad was the one who left him that ten thousand dollars he used for a down payment on the bakery. His name was Irv Sebran, and in the photo he looks a lot like Milt, though of course Milt wasn't born then—these four guys were teenagers or in their early twenties. Irv had one arm around his brother Carl, the worried-looking guy in the picture, and the other arm around Uncle Aaron. Anyway, Carl and Irv Sebran had some sort of falling out, but all Nathan knows is that it had something to do with the Bakers Union.

I'm not sure Milt ever even saw his father after the age of three, when Irv and Milt's mother divorced. I'll have to ask him when I get home. Nathan said Irv married again and had three girls with the second wife—they'd be Milt's half sisters. Turns out Irv was wildly successful running the family business and all three girls' families now own and operate several bagel outlets in the New York area. Nathan has business connections with them and occasionally socializes with Tom Sebran, son of one of the three sisters. He promised me he'd talk to Tom soon.

I have no idea if this has anything to do with Milt's predicament, but even if it doesn't, it's something I'd love to hear more about just because of Stu's family connection.

More when I get home.

chapter
15

....

I've been back home for thirty-six hours now and I feel as though I'd never left town. I'm not sure which is worse—the week before or the week after a trip. As crazed as I am trying to get away in the first place, I dread even more that bleak no-man's-land between coming and going, peopled only by unopened suitcases, crooked piles of mail drooping precariously on the kitchen table like yesterday's sand castles, and the blinking red eye of an overloaded answering machine.

Oy Vay isn't speaking to me after her long boarding stint at the vet's. I rouse myself from a jet-lagged stupor to make peace, and we slump together on the not-too-clean kitchen floor, each comforted by the other's body. Hot body, I should say. The air conditioner refuses to catch up from nine days off. There was a time I would have left it running thermostatically subdued, but now that I'm watching each penny that might help me keep my house, I don't waste the electricity. I know computers and Central Texas summers are mutually incompatible, but I take the chance.

I love this house. Old neighborhoods in Eternal are blessedly haphazard, meaning that Oy Vay can happily fertilize the green lawns of an aging mansion and the scrubby soil of a tiny gingerbread house on the same outing down our block. Our home is one size larger than gingerbread—two small stories plus the attic, with a front yard only big enough for roses and a backyard where I practically live when it's not too hot. For me, the weather's almost never too cold, so I'm outside in three seasons. Of course, I'm all too aware on a sweltering day like today that the summer season takes up half the year.

I haven't called Milt. What I should have done was to call him from New York when I was energized, but now I'm thinking I owe him a conversation free of this unaccustomed depression. Oh, and on top of everything else, I miss Joshie more than ever now that I've been together with him for more than a week. I'm sure this would only make sense to another mother, but Oy Vay nods as if she gets it.

Tonight I'll call Milt. Right now, while I'm still lying on the floor with my dog for support, I'm curious to return one of the many calls on my answering machine—one from Turner Goldman's secretary. I hope it's not bad news.

Well, it's not exactly bad. The main part of the message is good, actually. Good for Milt. Not good for one of Turner's partners, who had a stroke, causing an uproar in the office, causing Turner to ask the police for some extra time. I try to feel sorry for the stroke guy, a stranger to me, at the same time that I'm relieved for Milt, but I can't manage it, so I put the lapse on my mental confessional list—the one I'd refer to weekly if I were a Catholic. Not being one, I save this particular transgression for annual review.

Turner is in Oklahoma, filling in for the sick partner at a long trial. So far so good. But the legal secretary, one Bettyanne Riley-Silverberg—those chain-ganged surnames can be mini-dramas in themselves—now proceeds to rat-a-tat out a long but important addendum to Turner's message. She has obviously saved this for last so she can make a quick getaway. Turner is clearly calling in one of the many lifetime markers I owe him for accepting Milt as a not-all-that-solvent client. Besides, he says, he knows I'll want to be helpful re the stroke. Yep.

By this time, I'm unconsciously digging my nails into Oy Vay's back, and she wisely picks up her three legs and moves to the other side of the kitchen. I could swear she's got a gleam in her eye seeing me on the rack. It's payback time for the nine days at Bark 'n Board.

Turner Goldman, I'm told by Ms. Riley-Silverberg, is the co-chair with Mrs. Essie Sue Margolis for the Queen Esther Statue Fund-Raising Ball and Rabbinical Installation. It's formal.

No, Mr. Goldman *was* the co-chair. *Was* the co-chair. Ms. Riley-Silverberg makes that quite clear. In Turner's absence, the temple board, at his suggestion, has appointed me the co-chair—the justification being, I assume, that a rabbinical installation has the word *rabbi* in it and I am the local expert on all things rabbinical since I'm the widow of one. Mrs. Essie Sue Margolis, my co-chair, will take the entire Queen Esther Fund-Raising Ball off my hands and I need not worry about that—only the installation. I'm so gratified at this bit of news that I become ravenously hungry, but in a fit of prescience, Oy Vay has moved her Milk-Bone to the other side of the room.

Three computer clients had left me messages when I called the machine by remote from New York. Checking on those systems will take at least half the week to come. This is one of those times I'm glad business isn't so good, and I wonder once again if it would be doable to take on the partnership with Milt. Hey, at least I wouldn't starve. On the other hand, I tend to be unrealistic about the projects I take on, and before I know it, I'm overloaded.

I can see that this Twilight of the Nods on my kitchen floor might not be the best time to decide the rest of my life. Even slight jet lag seems to bring up all the oppressive problems I usually avoid as a queen of denial.

I'm mulling over a more important subject—whether wrinkles that have been in a suitcase for two days will be any harder to hang out than wrinkles in a suitcase for three days, when the phone rings and cuts off my reverie. I don't like the sound of it. Oy Vay looks over at me with a *so, nu?* expression and challenges me to answer it. Not wanting to add to the outrageous number of calls already on my machine, I pick it up.

"Ruby, darling, it's so good to hear your voice again."

Essie Sue. I haven't said hello yet, but that's all right. My expectations aren't high here—a good thing, because she keeps going.

"And how was the bar mitzvah? Did your nephew memorize his Portion well?"

I hesitate—not sure if Essie Sue has finished *her* Portion yet. She has a way of conversationally colliding with me whenever I think it's my turn to speak.

"It was a family birthday. Stu's Uncle Aaron turned eighty this—"

"Oh, the old four score and seven. He should only be well."

I think she has Genesis and the Gettysburg Address confused here, but who's counting?

"Yes, he's eighty. Thank you for the good wishes," I say on behalf of our family.

"He should also live to be a hundred and twenty, in the biblical sense."

"Right."

I can barely hold up the phone in this heat, much less play the Margolis version of *Can You Top This?* so I lie prone and wait for whatever will come. Plenty comes.

Skipping mercilessly from the Bible to her Filofax, she recites a list of nine dates she has blocked out for planning meetings.

"I suggest you use capital R slash capital B on your calendar," she begins, "to represent Rabbinical Installation slash Fund-Raising Ball. This way, we'll both be on the same wavelength throughout."

Throughout what? I wonder. She's dictating my abbreviations, yet?

"It's a rush job," she explains. "I've only scheduled nine meetings because we have to be finished with this whole *megillah* before Rosh Hashanah," she tells me. "By Rosh Hashanah, he's got to be totally installed.

You're not supposed to have him get up there on the High Holy Days uninstalled."

I think silently that the man's not some brand of dishwasher, but I keep blasphemous thoughts to myself. West Point would be jealous of the military campaign Essie Sue's got us embarking on.

"You're in charge of working with the rabbi and reporting to me so we can coordinate," she says. "He has to have another clergyman install him, of course. See if he has any rabbinical friends who would be willing to come in for the affair, or if we want to be cutting edge, we can have someone interfaith do it—like the episcopal bishop."

"Why don't we let him decide all that?" The campaign is going too fast for me. I also want to know why we're having the fund-raising ball right after. Are people supposed to come to the service in formal gowns? She informs me this part has all been worked out at the board meeting, and I'm not to bother myself with the order of service.

As a last attempt, I throw in the suggestion that since the rabbi was hired to be in charge of worship services, he should have the final word on the installation. Thanks to Essie Sue, I'm thinking Maytag every time I say that word.

At that, the monologue ends abruptly. Essie Sue never says good-bye—she just hangs up. As far as I know, no one has ever called her on it. We're all too grateful for the reprieve.

I suck an ice cube and pass one to Oy Vay. Vacation's over. I'm home.

chapter
16

....

I slip through the back door of The Hot Bagel just after lunch, so I can have some quiet time with Milt. He didn't answer last night when I called, and I'm worried—needlessly, I'm sure. The last thing I expect is to walk in on a fight.

At first, I think it's horseplay. Carol Sealy, the assistant cashier, has Gus Stamish, the head baker, spread-eagled across one of the big wooden flouring tables near the ovens. She's all muscle, from her long, athletic arms to her solid calves. This is a woman who works out—no doubt about it. Gus is pinned down in the middle, his own long arms and legs flailing about like a spider poked with a stick. His white hat is on the floor and is being stomped on by Carol as she shouts every name in the book at him.

"Take it back, you S.O.B. Take back what you said."

Gus is in no condition to take back anything, except

maybe a couple of croaky breaths while she's diverted by his other body parts.

Milt is nowhere to be seen, and I remember his parking space in back was empty. Fortunately, no one else is in the bakery.

"Hey, give it up!" Never one for confrontations, my own shouts are weak in comparison with Carol's, and she totally ignores me.

"You're choking me," Gus yelps when he gets some air. "Quit it!"

He acquires a modicum of strength from somewhere, and manages a half roll on top of her, leveraging his long-drink-of-water body so that Carol is now partially pinned down herself. It seems to be a draw for the present, and I try mere words again.

"Milt'll fire both of you when I tell him. Don't you need your jobs?" Ever the practical one, I figure this argument would move *me*. I don't know about them. Apparently, I'm a genius, because they both stop as if they suddenly realize for the first time there could be consequences from this fracas. Stunned, they sit up and look at me with blank expressions, sweat dripping from their faces.

"It's unbelievable a customer hasn't walked in here in the middle of this," I say.

"It's her fault. She jumped me for no reason." Gus is still out of breath.

"My fault? You accused me of stealing." Carol seems none the worse for wear.

"I've been watching her," he says to me as he picks his hat off the floor.

"Yeah, your eyes are all over me all the time, you creep. You have the beady eyes of one of those serial killers."

"I watch her a lot. She's been taking money out of the cash register to ruin Milt. As bad as we've been grossing these days, too. We need the money."

"What's with the we?" Carol yells. "It's not your store."

"And it's not yours. Do you think you can just stick your hand in the cookie jar and help yourself?"

"Okay, break it up, guys." They're moving closer to each other, and I'm afraid they'll start up all over again. "I'm sure Milt checks the receipts." I start to say more but a little voice tells me to wait for Milt. For all I know, he's so preoccupied he's forgetting to run the place with his usual business sense.

"Don't be so sure," Gus stammers. "He's not himself these days."

"Who's not himself these days?"

Gus and Carol do a double take before I can turn around.

"Hi, boss." Carol, to my utter amazement, flashes a smile. I also notice she's hardly rumpled from the brawl. What a recovery. Gus, on the other hand, looks like something the cat dragged in—shirt totally out of his pants and fingernail scratches from eye to cheek.

"My God, what happened to you?" Milt, actually looking better than he had before I left, hurries to Gus with a look of concern while Carol hooks her arm into his and pulls him off to the side. I can't believe she's going to try to put a spin on what happened when I'm standing here as a witness.

The front door opens and a group of four customers comes in, so we put everything on hold. Milt heads toward them, the Terrible Twosome stay in the back glaring at each other, and I scratch my head trying to decide how much to spill to Milt, despite my previous threats to tell all. One thing seems perfectly clear to me, though. This place needs supervision. And I'm wondering what's the deal with the Gus and Carol story.

Later in the afternoon I do get to sit down with Milt in relative privacy at a table by the front window. He's definitely distracted, because he doesn't seem to get it that this was a real fight I stumbled into.

"They've never liked each other," he says. He thinks Gus is weirder than Carol, and pooh-poohs the thought that she may be stealing. "Why now? She's worked here for years and I've never had a problem with her." He promises to have Grace keep a good account of the end-of-day receipts, and I talk him into letting me take the books more often to the freelance bookkeeper he uses, instead of waiting for the woman to show up in her own good time. I use our possible partnership as a way to ease him into more accountability.

"You don't want me buying into a business that's not there, do you?"

"Are you really considering this? In light of everything that's about to happen to me?"

"Yep. I never did make great money choices. But I know in my gut you'll be back here in full force before the year's out."

"Well, if the worst happens, you'll be running the place for both of us."

Not with your present delightful staff, I tell myself.

But to Milt I say, "Then *I'll* get to make the millions from bagels. Either way, we'll be okay."

I'm also hesitant to press too much about the case. I had hoped to pump Turner for all that, not Milt. But I'm too curious not to push a little.

"I don't mind talking about it, Ruby," Milt says. "Turner thinks the case is weak on motivation, but with the circumstantial evidence they've got, that might not matter. Even the police don't seem that convinced about the case, but they're not looking around much for the real killer. We've got an investigator working on other leads. I've cashed in some retirement funds to pay him, and Turner's been a brick about not asking for money up front."

"What other leads? What's the guy found?"

"Nothing, but he hasn't been working for us that long. Turner's convinced this is a frame—that Marla was killed to get me."

"So why weren't you killed instead if someone hated you that much?"

"I don't know."

He's looking morose again, and I realize I've gone too far. I want to be a comfort to him, not the Angel of Death hovering around him. I change the subject and talk about the New York trip. Here, too, though, I'm not sure how far to go. If Milt's mother didn't tell him that much about his father's family, maybe he's not going to be exactly thrilled to learn about the second wife, three daughters, and the roaring success of Irv's business. I'm dealing with a friend's life here, and I have to be careful. I start with the sepia photo and tell him I saw an early photo of his father. He perks up.

"So tell me more. This is what I kept noodging Stu to find out about. My mother would never talk about my dad. I didn't want to push it because it seemed to make her sad, and my real dad didn't think it was a good idea."

"Your real dad?"

"I know it sounds backward, but in my heart, my real dad has always been Hank Aboud, who adopted me. He's the one I called Daddy, and my birth father, Irv Sebran, was just a name to me. Yeah, he did leave me ten thousand when he died and Mom seemed pleased, but he never wanted to see me or even to write to me, so the inheritance was like winning the lottery or something—not that real. But I'm as curious as the next guy, and of course I wanted to know about Irv Sebran."

I lay it all out for him—the business success, the possible feud, and the second family, even down to Tom, who'd be Milt's half nephew. I tell him Tom is Nathan's friend and that the two young guys are going to find out more about the falling out between the two brothers— Milt's father Irv and Carl Sebran.

He's thrilled that Nathan is going to make a print for him of the sepia photo of the four friends. And I'm happy that I can give him something good to think about for a change. At least I hope it's good.

chapter
17

....

I emerge onto the Julius Y. Levy patio on the dot of seven, knowing I won't be afforded the luxury of sitting behind the real players. Tonight, thanks to my friend Turner, I am one of the players. In my official capacity as co-chair of the "R Slash B," I'm only hoping I can get through the night without slashing my own wrists. I can see Essie Sue rustling papers at the head of a long folding table set up on the patio.

The Levy patio was added to the Temple as an after-thought in 1960 when there were no more rooms to be named and the Levy family insisted on a piece of the architecture. Julius's full-length portrait, over protests that I won't go into, was affixed to the Texas limestone wall at the back of the building and now overlooks all outdoor weddings, receptions, and youth group basket-ball games. In the portrait he stands in front of his shoe store on Main Street, one of the oldest establishments in Eternal. The artist has painted his tie askew, just as it always was in real life. Stately, he's not, but there's a great gleam in his eye—no doubt because he knew something his competitors didn't. On his feet are black sneakers—high tops, in fact. Main Street thought he was a *meshuganah* when he suddenly had a Going About My Business sale and got rid of every single dress shoe in the place. Within seven years he became the athletic shoe king of Central Texas, or as he used to say, "I knew from Nikes before Nikes knew from themselves."

In a church down on the South Texas border there's a bona fide religious portrait that draws pilgrims because it displays real tears. Julius's portrait seems to be perspiring right here on the patio, and tonight I'm a believer. Why anyone would schedule a committee meeting outside on such a humid night is beyond me. We're all fanning away. The evening breeze is nonexistent—in fact, there's an antibreeze—a kind of black hole sucking in the air and making it impossible to breathe.

When our temple only had fifty families in the 1920s, the congregants used to borrow fans from the only funeral home in the county. That they were Jesus fans was unfortunate. Once when we had a visiting rabbi, he instructed that the fans be waved with the funeral home ads facing him, and the rows of Jesus heads facing the congregation. He felt outnumbered, I guess. But even he would never have dared suggest that the fans be dispensed with. The town of Eternal marked the far edge of the *real* South—it belonged with the wet bayous of East Texas and Louisiana, not the dry hills of the west. Fans kept southerners alive in those days, and you took them where you could get them.

Essie Sue's makeup is running as she calls the meeting to order. I'm surprised she puts up with having to wipe her mascara in public, but she seems determined to get this meeting moving.

"Ladies and gentlemen, we have no time to lose in preparing for this momentous event."

I notice she calls everything an event. It's weird. Her life seems to move from event to event—unlike mine. Life between events is the part I can't seem to get enough of.

As her partner, I get introduced first. She then proceeds to pass out stapled packets to each member of the committee. This must be a mega-event in her panoply of major happenings, because she has summoned a dozen people here. I wonder if half are mine, but as a mere co-chair I haven't been briefed. I used to be bothered by these things, but as the years go by, I find that going with the flow is the only way to survive—especially when Turner's the one who should be sitting here bathed in sweat. I'm sure that soon more will be revealed to me than I care to co-chair.

Kevin's not here. I lean over and ask Essie Sue where he is, but she's tight-lipped. "The rabbi will join us in due course."

Essie Sue has requested that Brother be on the committee, but she's gotten Buster instead. She's not pleased.

"Who paid for all this paper?" he says, waving his stack. "And who has time to read all this material? This looks like the annual report from IBM."

"I'm nothing if not organized, Mr. Copeland. And the

agendas will be paid for out of the funds raised for this event."

"That means we're already in debt for the agendas," Buster says. "I warned you I was coming here with a calculator." At that he flashes a Hewlett-Packard pocket analyzer. "You know how I feel about your grand designs, Essie Sue. They suck up money this temple doesn't have."

"*Au contraire*, Buster," she says, apparently abandoning the Mister. She's known him since grammar school. "This temple wouldn't be alive without my fund-raisers. Remember the production of 1977, when we brought the celebrities in?"

"You mean the one everybody got rich off of but the Temple?"

I stand up. "We're getting off track here. How many people want to stick to the nineties?"

Ten hands go up. Essie Sue glares, but I figure I'm entitled as a co-. We're lucky we got off with just the seventies.

The rest of the hour is spent with everyone going over the agendas, page by page. Actually, Essie Sue *should* be running IBM. The woman is, as she says, nothing if not organized. Each of the committee members is in charge of a "fund-raising segment." That means they hound people only twice by phone and then report the slackers back to Essie Sue.

"Two turndowns means they're not phone material," she tells us. "You pay one personal, informal visit on your own."

"A personal, informal visit means you catch 'em with no warning?" Buster hasn't given up yet.

She ignores him. "One personal, informal visit on your own, and then report back to me. No more. And by the way, before we adjourn later tonight, I'm passing around a piece of paper to take pledges from all the committee."

Arthur Fine of the Brotherhood raises his hand. "So what happens when we report the no-givers back to you after the personal, informal visits?"

"You don't have to worry about them anymore. I'll take the hard cases."

All eyes go to the right and then to the left, as if to memorize our fellow committee members who might not make it.

I notice everyone signs the pledge paper when it's passed around.

Essie Sue explains her position on the hard cases.

"Look," she says, regretfully speaking down to us innocents, "there are two kinds of hard cases. The first won't give to anything. The second will give—they merely haven't met their match yet. They consider themselves pushovers if they give in to just anyone. So they wait for someone more—uh—assertive, and then it becomes a negotiation. This type is insulted if they're approached by someone wimpier than they are, see?"

We bow to her superior knowledge. I've personally always been in awe of people like Essie Sue who can take on the hard cases. Maybe it is a power play, but if so, they go where the rest of us fear to tread, and we benefit from it. She's not finished educating us, though.

"The core givers begin the process—they're in a whole class by themselves. The core givers are the big ones, and they're interested in one of two things. Usu-

ally, they want to promote a good cause they consider worthy. If they're not interested in that, then they're interested in one another. Part of the responsibility of being a core giver is that you kick in when the givers who are equal to you kick in. When another giver has a pet project, you don't look the other way."

Even Buster seems fascinated, but he can't resist an *utz* anyway. "We know about the top group," he says, "but the next group is harder. The top group at least *wants* the particular good work, whatever it happens to be."

Buster gets a pitying look from our teacher. "You're dead wrong," she says. "The next group is the easiest. The next group under the top givers is curious about the top givers. Have one of them open a home or chair a committee, and the next group will be there."

Arthur Fine raises his hand. "But can't we just put the idea out there and trust that if the cause is good, people will support it?"

"No. That's like reaching half your audience. Half will come to you to support a good cause, and the other half you have to come to."

At that, she nods her head toward the doorway, as if on cue. She never segues from one subject to another— like her phone calls, when she's finished, she's finished.

"Come in, Rabbi." Kevin appears with a big stack of folded tee shirts in his arms.

"We have to get with it, people—and this little surprise will serve as a great motivational tool."

I should think Essie Sue's all the motivational tool one committee can take, but apparently not. She whips a shirt from the top of the pile in Kevin's arms and holds it up before us. It's a cartoon figure of one huge sumo wrestler—the victor, sitting on top of another—the vanquished. The caption reads, "Give Till It Hurts."

I don't think so. "You want us to wear these things," I say, "or are they gifts for contributors like the tote bags on public TV?"

"We wear them, of course." If looks could kill, I'd be on the slab already. "They're for each member of our committee. They're bound to stir up conversation, and people will be able to identify us. Like product identification. Believe me, this works."

"Are you kidding?" Buster asks. "They'll run for cover if they have two cents' worth of brains in their heads. And how much did this crap cost?"

"It was a contribution. A goodwill contribution from the tee-shirt place in the mall. He had these extra sumo shirts that didn't sell and after I persuaded him, he agreed to give them to us."

I'd like to have been a fly on the wall during that little encounter.

"The rabbi was helpful enough to go to the warehouse to pick them up for us—they'd been sent back from the mall already."

Yeah, scheduled for oblivion. Obviously, Essie Sue fobbed this job off on the unsuspecting Kevin.

Born to please. I've gotta give him lessons. Quick.

But first, I move that we vote this down—wearing those shirts is all we'd need. I win the majority—thank heavens for small favors. Not that I'd be caught dead in one of them, but I've learned the hard way that Essie Sue's followers take instructions literally.

"Maybe the unfortunate can use them," she says, glaring at me.

"You mean, the less fortunate?" Buster says. "*We're* the unfortunate."

I squeeze a seat for Kevin by me. I'm definitely not looking for a footsie opportunity, I hasten to add. I just figure this should save me a few phone calls down the line.

"Kevin, don't you think you should start planning your installation instead of getting so involved in Essie Sue's ideas for the fund-raiser?"

When he gives me a look like a deer frozen in the headlights, I realize he's caught between loyalties. He wants to let off steam, but he can't exactly trust me. This I understand completely. He's new to this place, and the worst thing he could possibly do is start confiding in the wrong person. When a new rabbi comes to town, suddenly everyone wants to be his best friend. Some of these best friends are gonna get him into big trouble before he sorts them out. I have a new respect for Kevin—at least he's smart enough to be wary.

"Oh no," he says. "I volunteered to help Essie Sue. And I didn't appreciate the motion you just passed, after all our hard work. She's asked me to call her Essie Sue instead of Mrs. Margolis. I think that speaks for itself friendship-wise, don't you?"

I backtrack for a minute. "I'm glad you're getting along so well. It's just that I'm sure she'll understand that you might delegate some of these duties to other people on the committee in order to take care of your own priorities."

"But, my dear Ruby, you don't understand. Her priorities are my priorities. Mrs. Margolis—I mean Essie Sue—*made* this congregation. She told me so. What better example could I follow?" He leans over and whispers in my ear. "She also told me that under the right influence, your own somewhat wayward attitudes could be shaped to excellent service as . . ."

"Whoa." I sit bolt upright. Am I dreaming, or did the deer in the headlights just rear up on its hind legs and bite me?

I don't even get a chance to lick my wounds and reconnoiter. Essie Sue's wagging finger is turned our way. "Now, now. I think I just caught our Rabbi Kapstein and our Ruby giggling in the corner there. Precious as that is, I can't let your little dalliance interrupt our meeting."

Kevin beams at me. Or is it a leer? At any rate, he caps it with a wink at Essie Sue. What am I supposed to say now? That I resent the word dalliance? That we weren't giggling? I never got this right in sixth grade, much less now. One thing I do remember—I always protested too much, calling even more attention to myself.

I'm smarter now. Ignoring the little voice inside that says, yeah, sure you are, I stand up and take the deer by the antlers.

"Essie Sue's right," I say. "We've been here an hour and a half already. I'd like to appoint a committee to help Kevin with his installation service."

Kevin jumps up beside me. "I'm sure you meant to say Rabbi Kapstein, not Kevin," he says. "And I understood very firmly from Mrs. Margolis that you were to help me with the service. I see no need at all to waste the valuable time of a number of people when you and I will have the situation well in hand."

"No," I insist, "I think you need the input of a number of people. I'd like to see a show of hands." I'm actually asking these people to volunteer themselves for another committee? Yeah, I've really learned a lot since sixth grade. No hands go up, of course, and Kevin sits down, looking smug.

Essie Sue is radiant as she calls the meeting to a close. "Thank you, Rabbi Kapstein, for setting us all straight. Sometimes it's very difficult to take charge all alone. I've been waiting for years," she says with a sad look at me, "to find someone brave enough to jump into the fray and take control when circumstances call for it."

"My dear Essie Sue, you've found your helpmate," Kevin says.

"And you've just lost yours," I mutter as I pass in front of him. He doesn't hear me because he's dealing with my full glass of iced tea that happened to fall in his lap.

chapter
18

....

I narrowly avoid hitting any cars on the way home,
which is a miracle considering I'm slitty-eyed with evil
thoughts from my ordeal at the meeting. I can hear my
phone ringing as I pull into the garage, and I run in and
grab it just before the answering machine goes on.

"Hi, Ruby, it's your cousin Nathan from New York."

"Hey, Nathan, what's happening, dude?"

I'm suddenly light-headedly happy, just realizing
there's life beyond committees. Nathan makes me feel
good, and I've missed him. I take the phone over to the
sofa and plop.

"I've been playing private eye, just like I said I
would."

"I'm all ears. Where did you start?"

"First I made contact with Tom again. I told you he's
Irv Sebran's grandson, but I wasn't sure which of the
three daughters was his mother—I get 'em all mixed up.

Turns out he's the oldest daughter's kid, and she's a few years older than her sisters. She was old enough to remember Irv's brother Carl before he died, and she knows people who keep her posted on Carl's widow. The widow's old—she's my grandfather's generation."

"So did you call her?"

"I did better than that. Tom's mom said the old woman wouldn't be any good over the phone—she doesn't hear well. So Tom and I took the train out to New Jersey and dropped in at the bakery their family still runs."

"I thought the family had a whole chain of bakeries in the New York area."

"No, no, Ruby. Only one brother's side owns all the bakeries. Irv Sebran's daughters—one of them being Tom's mother, as I said—run twelve bagel outlets all over the city. Carl Sebran's family only has this one place in Jersey City. My grandpa Aaron knows something about Carl and Irv, but I can't seem to get it out of him. He says he made promises way back not to talk about the Sebran family's secrets."

"Let's leave him out of it, then. So what did you find out when you visited?" Oy Vay's up on the sofa beside me, mashing the breath out of my chest cavity. I guess she's interested.

"Carl died of cancer several years ago. His widow's name is Ida Sebran. She's eighty, like Grandpa. I was surprised when Tom told me she still goes to work, and even more surprised to see how vigorous she is. She's a little woman, hard and thin like a prune, with her hair skinned back in a bun. She's very bitter, though, just like Tom says Carl always was."

Nathan talks for more than half an hour, even over my protests that he should hang up and let me call him back on my dime.

"Next time," he says.

I find out from Nathan that Ida goes to work every day because her two grown kids, Henry and Celia, have both taken off for greener fields. She told Nathan they left the only legacy their father could give them, and she's working to save it for them when they decide to come back home. Not that it sounds like much to save. Ida, Carl, and their children had a hard life together, struggling to earn a livelihood from the bakery, and feeling entirely cut off from Carl's brother and the rest of the family.

Ida wouldn't tell why the brothers broke up. She only said that every day of their lives, she and the children were spoon-fed Carl's bitterness and resentment.

Tom asked if he and Nathan could come to see the old lady again, but she didn't exactly pull out the welcome mat.

"All in all," Nathan tells me at the end of the conversation, "it was frustrating, but I didn't have a bad feeling about the visit. Tom and I both want to know that part of the family history, and actually, Tom's mother is pushing for us to find out, too. Carl's children would be her cousins, and she'd like to meet them. Maybe if we can figure out another excuse to see her, we can get her to show us a family album."

From the phone I go to e-mail. What a world. I'm revved up from Nathan's information, however meager, about Carl and his children, and I doubt if I could fall asleep before midnight, anyway. I find a note from Nan and it's not good.

E-mail from: Nan
To: Ruby
Subject: *It's Berke or Me*

I absolutely cannot stand one more minute of this job. Stanford P. Jerk, Esquire, has jerked me around for the last time. I'm a mere legal secretary and he's got me writing briefs for him, which is fine because it's not half as boring as filing motions for him. I'm also savvy to the ways of the world, and the fact that he pays me sixteen an hour for something he charges the client two hundred fifty an hour for is also okay by me, since I know he's got the bar certification, not me. He was having Ben, the last law clerk, write the briefs, but he discovered I was helping Ben do the research and writing, so when Ben went back to school he asked me to do it.

Anyway, now the Berke Jerk has turned down my modest-by-any-standard request for a raise to put me where the other legal secretaries are. He says he can't afford it. I feel totally stuck. If I get another job, which would not be that hard, I'll be back to doing the usual legal secretarial bit, and I don't think I can stand it. Granted, Vicki's in her last year of college and I've made it through that financial morass, but all that really means is that now we both have debts.

Sorry for the downer. Don't deal with it if you're overloaded. Anything new with Milt?

E-mail from: Ruby
To: Nan
Subject: *Are We Really Dancing This Dance Again?*

I hate to do this, but who else in your life can you count on to stomp all over you when you're down? Look—I feel awful that jerko Berke isn't giving you the raise—I really do, hon. But basically, you've put the whole problem in a nutshell all by yourself. What you're saying to me illustrates perfectly what I've been telling you since time immemorial. You're selling yourself short.

I understood when you decided to stay home and help Jim with the accounting part of the business while Vicki was little. But Jim's long gone, Vicki's not little, and where are you?

It's perfectly obvious to me that you get a real thrill out of anything in your job that requires some creative legal reasoning. You talk to me about cases and the whole screen comes alive. So will you really end up applying for another job as legal secretary, or even worse, take the raise Berke'll eventually offer you just when he senses you're serious about leaving?

There's an equation missing here. You were the accounting major. You do the math.

....

E-mail from: Nan
To: Ruby
Subject: *It's Too Big a Step*

You're suggesting law school, right? I've just finished getting Vicki through school and I just don't think I can deal with the expense this would create in my life.

I'm forty-five years old, I'd have to work while I was in school in order to make it and you know how difficult law school is to begin with, I've heard the LSAT is a horrible ordeal, and lastly, I don't have the energy after dealing with Berke.

•••

E-mail from: Ruby
To: Nan
Subject: *Law School*
   Think about it.

•••

E-mail from: Ruby
To: Nan
Subject: *P.S.*

Forgot to answer your question about the latest on Milt. His mother lives down in Port Aransas, on the coast about three to four hours from here. We're driving down there tomorrow morning and coming back at night—neither of us has time to make a two-day trip out of it. He's been telling me for a couple of years now that she's getting senile, so I figured she was out as a resource. He's also been terribly reticent about bringing up the past to her. But Turner called me yesterday and strongly suggested we go down there to see if she might come up with something that will help. He doesn't trust Milt to do the kind of thorough digging we really need here, so he thought my brand of terrier-dogging might do the trick. It won't matter, of course, if she's really out of it.
   More later.

chapter
19

....

I go through the back door to the bakery, leaving my car in Milt's parking lot so he can do the driving in his catering van. It's huge, and is much safer on the highway than my little peanut, which usually ends up being the Ping-Pong ball between two behemoths playing chicken. At least in the van we have a fighting chance.

Actually, the highway down to the coast is one of the safer routes, and I'm looking forward to it. It's a relaxing drive right through the heart of Texas history. You wouldn't know, from driving by the corn- and cotton-fields, that armies were massacred there in the Texas fight for independence from Mexico. The rural landscape is almost too peaceful to accommodate all those ghosts. I get a discombobulated feeling whenever I try to reconcile the land and the legend.

Milt is in the back room, putting together a little breakfast-to-go. Piping hot rye bagels, with cream cheese for schmearing—that'll be my job in the passenger seat. Hot black coffee for both of us and a pint of cold orange juice. Yum.

Three of the regulars are prepared to take over for the day. The former pugilists, Carol and Gus, are peaceful enough, and to the mix is added Bradley Axelrod, who seems awfully inquisitive for someone whose mind is supposed to be up in the air chasing numbers. Apparently, Milt has filled them all in on our little trip. I had thought he might want to keep it confidential, but what do I know? Turner didn't tell us to keep it a secret. On the other hand, I thought it was supposed to be about *unloosing* past secrets, and I don't think I'd have let the whole store in on it. Especially these three, whom Milt seems to regard almost like family. The Addams Family, in my humble opinion.

I take the deep breath that's supposed to remind me I can't control what other people do. I learned this from a visiting therapist hired by one of the companies whose computer systems I'm paid to keep humming. One of my little corporate obligations was to attend a stress relief seminar. The brochure I got in the mail made it sound like flood relief, so it almost got put in the wrong pile until I noticed a handwritten request (read that *demand*) from the owner of the company that I attend with his compliments. Having learned from bitter experience that these types are much more sensitive about their obligatory communal forays into touchy-feely land than they are about their software, I showed up.

What I learned, aside from the fact that I can't wrap myself into those lopsided desks with the Ping-Pong paddle arms anymore, was that I'm a control freak. Batteries of soul-numbing multiple-choice tests told me so.

As did the teacher, who preferred to be known as our facilitator.

My lifelong curiosity about anything and anybody, which I admit got me P (Poor) in Conduct on all my elementary school report cards, at least made life interesting. But this is not a good thing, as the P's should have told me, had I been paying attention. My facilitator, who looked startlingly like all the schoolteachers who thought I wasn't living up to my potential, anointed me a C Type.

The reason we C Types want to know so much is so we can Direct the Outcome. The A Types are Authentically Integrated (the goody-goodies are still making A's, I notice); the B Types are—Boring? No. They're Basically Balanced—not as good as the A's, but of course better than the C's. The C Types like me have the most potential, though. For strokes, heart attacks, and nervous breakdowns. I don't believe our facilitator said nervous breakdown—I think it was something more politically correct, like Prozac Challenged. What we're supposed to do is quit absorbing so much information. When we're happily hot on the trail of something, we should stop and take a deep breath. When we exhale, hopefully, we'll lose the scent.

I'm taking a deep breath now so as not to worry that Bradley, Carol, and Gus know all about our trip to the coast.

Bradley is taking a fresh batch of bagels out of the ovens and dumping them into the big glass bins under the counters. "So I don't get it," Bradley says to me. "How come *you're* going to see the old lady?"

"My mother is Mrs. Aboud to you," Milt says.

"Ruby's going along to take notes for me. We want to see if Mom remembers anything about the old days back in New York."

"Why?"

If Milt thinks Bradley's going to stop now, he's crazy. Maybe I can fix this.

"We're just getting background," I say, and am instantly sorry. A question-stopper this isn't.

"Huh? Background for what?" Bradley's off and running.

I whisper to Milt that Grace isn't going to be too thrilled if we sit here and get a late start, and then don't return home until midnight. He bites.

"Okay, guys, back to work. Ruby and I can't yak all day with the staff. We have eight hours of driving back and forth."

Bradley's not happy. "I want to know what background from the old days has got to do with Marla Solomon's murder."

Hey, maybe Bradley's a C Type. Give these people too much information and you're dead.

chapter
20

....

The water at Port Aransas lacks the brilliant coloration of the sea farther south at Padre Island, but its more delicate hues still sparkle. I've always thought of it as one of the Gulf of Mexico's choicest goodies. Visual artists have taken to the special light that illuminates the shore—especially in the early morning hours.

"My mom was a painter," Milt tells me as we pull up to a small four-unit apartment a block from the beach. "We lived in Eternal most of my childhood, but she and my stepdad moved down here twenty years ago when he retired, so she could paint the seascapes she'd always wanted to do firsthand. Most of the artists are in Rockport a few miles away, but my dad loved this part of the coast, and that's where they settled in.

"She was a very vibrant woman until a few years ago. She's frail now, and her eyes aren't good. Thank God she can't read newspapers," he says almost as an after-thought. "She's never been a TV watcher, either, and she doesn't know about all my trouble."

We're expected. A large woman with heavy coils of black hair piled on top of her head answers our knock and gives Milt a hug.

"Ruby, this is my cousin Sara. She and Mom share the apartment and Sara watches over her."

"A harder job than it used to be," Sara says as she leads us into a tiny bedroom. Milt's mother sits in a narrow chaise lounge near the window. There's hardly room for it beside the twin beds which fill the remainder of the space. She herself doesn't take up much room— I'd say she weighs ninety-five pounds on a good day. I know from Milt that she's seventy-seven. That's old, but not as old as the late seventies used to be—I see a lot of very active people her age. This woman, though, is old.

Milt is beaming, and kneels down to kiss her cheek. "Mom," he says, "this is my friend Ruby—the one Grace and I talked about last time we were down here. I've brought her to visit you. Ruby, this is my mother, Anna Aboud."

It's obvious these two are close—she seems as happy to see him as he is to see her. Milt has told me he'd move her up to Eternal in a minute if she'd come, but she won't give up living at the beach. Cousin Sara pushes her wheelchair to the water every good day. "She's light as a feather," Sara tells us, "and it's only the one block from our apartment to a view of the waves."

"But I can't paint them anymore. My hands tremble

with the brush." Anna is agitated, but Milt smooths her forehead.

"Sara, as long as we're here, would you like to take a break?"

"I'd love it. When shall I come back? She won't last talking for more than a half hour, if that, but if you're planning to stay longer, you might want to stay if she dozes off."

"Of course we'll stay. Why don't you take an hour or so? We'll be fine. Could we fix her lunch?"

Milt is such a love. So gentle. No wonder those employees of his run circles around him—he just can't conceive of not trusting people. The very idea of his being a murder suspect is so ludicrous I'm about to blow a gasket until I settle myself down by sampling a juicy strawberry from the fruit basket Sara's put beside us. I'm looking around at the walls, which are covered with Anna's seascapes—summer blues and turquoises and the brackish waves of winter.

"I'll come back to fix lunch," Sara says. "I'll need to dole out her noon medicine. If you can stay for lunch, I'll bring back something more from the grocery."

"We'll stay if she wants us," Milt says, "but if it's like other visits, an hour will be way more than she can take. And we're planning to have lunch later, thanks. I did bring along some food in the cooler for you."

"Deli and bagels?" Sara seems thrilled. "A treat, Anna," she says, and then turns to us. "Not that she'll touch any of it. But I will."

I'm happy to see Sara leave, now that I realize we'll have such a limited time to get any information from Milt's mom. I slip out the palm-sized spiral notebook I keep in my purse. I want to tape the conversation with the small tape recorder I've also tucked away, but Milt says no, so I don't push. He does seem hopeful, though, because his mother seems more alert than usual today.

"Mom, I want you to do me a favor. Remember you always told me you didn't want to talk much about the old days, but that someday you would? About my dad Irv's family? Neither one of us is getting any younger, you know, and I really feel it's part of my heritage. Will you answer some questions for me?"

"I remember more about those days sometimes than I do about what I did an hour ago, Miltie."

He looks at me and I nod *go*. He's getting no resistance, and we both realize, I think, what a small window of opportunity we have here. I sit on one of the beds and take notes while Milt sits on the floor cross-legged beside the chaise lounge. He holds his mother's hand.

"Do you remember your sister-in-law, Ida Sebran, Mom? The woman who was married to your first husband Irv's brother Carl? Back in New York before we came out here?"

The eyes look blank. I'm worried.

"Ida. Sure. Ida," she says. "This is a woman who would pin her broken slip strap with a safety pin as big as a man's thumb and wear it with a scoop neckline. If she was too lazy to sew the strap, why wouldn't she wear a round collar to hide it? Do you suppose she didn't care?"

This last is directed at me. I keep a straight face and try not to look at Milt. Senile? I don't think so.

"So, Anna," I plunge in, deciding to go for broke.

"Tell us about Ida and Carl. Were the four of you good friends?"

Milt looks horrified, but I figure this is just why Turner wanted me to go along. Milt could easily pussyfoot around until nap time, and besides, I have a gut feeling that if we approach this as delicate terrain, Anna might duck for cover.

"Friends? We were relatives. It's different. To tell you the truth, the woman got on my nerves."

I try another tack. "Were Irv and Carl close?"

"They were close until their father died. That was when my Milt was two years old. His grandfather Sebran passed away when he was only two."

"But, Mom, that was just a year before you and my dad divorced."

"That was a bad year, Miltie. My whole life changed that year."

"You never would talk to me about the divorce. About Dad at all, for that matter."

"Ida handed down only bitterness to her children over what happened. I didn't want to do the same thing to you. So I kept quiet."

"You made a mistake, Mom. He was my father. I need to know anything about him I can know."

This might be some form of clue-hunting to Turner and me, but I can see that Milt is now into it on a much deeper level.

"I meant to protect your memories of the family."

"Mom, I had no memories of the family."

"What happened, Anna?" I decide it's probably easier for her to direct the tough stuff to me. She and Milt are going to continue to pussyfoot.

Anna tilts her head back on the chaise pillow and closes her eyes—not restfully, but as if to summon all her energy and concentration.

"Your father fooled around a little bit, and this made me very unhappy. Carl knew about it, too. I was suspicious. But Irv told me he loved only me, and I believed him."

"This I can understand, Mom. I mean, I figured it was something like that. What would have been so hard to tell me?"

"The women suspicions I could have taken—at least for a while. People didn't talk divorce so fast in those days, and I had you to think about."

She's still dancing around something—I can tell. It must be something awfully hard to cough up.

"Don't worry about it, Mom. I can come to terms with that. Let's talk about something more pleasant."

I freeze. What's he doing? It comes to me pronto that he thinks that's it. That she just kept the running around from him.

"Yes, Milt. Let's talk about something else. Maybe you can wheel me by the water after I have my lunch."

I slide off the bed and go sit at the foot of the chaise lounge. I ignore Milt's glare.

"So what else did you want to protect Milt from, Anna?"

She stares at me with that look one woman can give another in a man's company—a look that says she realizes I have her number but Milt doesn't.

"I don't think I want to remember any more."

I'm positive Anna doesn't know about Milt's problems, but I'm trusting in her mother's instinct that something's wrong in his life, even if she doesn't want to know what it is.

"This is one of those times when remembering could help your son," I say as gently as I can.

She turns fully toward me. She's talking straight to me now, as if not looking at Milt can still protect him. And she's taking her time. I need to shut up.

"These boys, who were always such great buddies, fell out completely when their father died. The old man was proud of both his boys, and wanted them to share in the business when he died. He left it to both of them. Carl was the oldest, and had a special place in his father's heart because he was the young boy who had come over from Europe with them. He carried all the memories.

"My husband Irv was born a few years later, after the family had moved to New York. The brothers were raised to be close, and they were."

I shouldn't interrupt, but I can't resist telling her about the sepia photo of the four young men.

"I know that picture," she says. "They were still friends then. But the fighting started ten years later, after Carl and Irv had already married Ida and me. They just couldn't get along after their father died. Carl wanted to keep everything in the bakery the same—the way the old man had. Carl was always the cautious one. The same counters, the same kettles for boiling, the same old wood tables for the customers."

I offer Anna some water, but she waves it away. "Irv was more modern. He said it was 1948, not 1933. He had been in the Army—not overseas, but still he considered himself more sophisticated. He had big plans for bagels in New York after the war. He wanted Carl to go in with him to borrow money for a total makeover of the place—new tables, mirrored walls, shiny counters, and a modern kitchen. Carl was terrified of getting into debt, and he wouldn't hear of it.

"And they fought. All the time. Irv would come home to me and rant and rave, but Ida said Carl was worse— he would come home and brood. Finally, Irv had enough. He decided to go out on his own. He said staying together wasn't worth being miserable every day of his working life. I was scared about the money, but I supported him in the decision. You can get cancer from worrying too much. That's how Carl himself died a few years ago. He had cancer for years."

Milt is no longer sitting on the floor—he's pacing around. "So they broke up? Big deal." I can tell there's no way he wants to hear more. Maybe he has a premonition.

"Then what happened?" I keep my eyes locked to hers, hoping she'll go on.

"Irv opened a brand-new shop and attracted some younger customers. People started coming in for coffee and bringing their friends. I helped out at the cash register, and little Miltie ran around. It was a cute place, and Irv was happy. I wasn't so happy with his schmoozing the women customers, but I put up with it, and it didn't hurt business, either.

"One summer day, out of the blue, a man in a white suit and a Panama straw hat comes in and asks for Irv. He hands him a folded light blue paper. It turns out his own brother Carl is taking him to court for 'appropriating' their father's secret recipes."

Milt interrupts. "In the bagel business, Ruby, each bakery's formula for bagels was like gold. It's still true, although not as much as in those days. But, Mom—they were Irv's recipes, too, right?"

"Irv knew that right away. He says to me after we read the blue papers, 'I told you my brother was a little crazy in the head, Anna. He's jealous. He can't stand it that my business has taken off so well, and that the children of our old customers are more comfortable in my place. He's brought this crazy idea to some lawyer, who's taking him to the cleaners.'

"I was worried anyway," Anna said, "but it didn't seem to bother Irv. At first."

Anna asks to be brought back over to the bed, and we help her. I know we're tiring her and part of me doesn't want to, but the other part knows this could be important. As I help lift Anna onto the bed, I'm trying to sneak a look at my watch without Milt's seeing me. I'm afraid he'll quit too soon. It doesn't take long, though, for me to realize that he's as hooked as I am. He's not even thinking about the time.

Anna finally drinks some water and settles down.

"Then the troubles started," she says, "just like my worst fears. When families get set against each other, everything elevates."

"Escalates," Milt says.

"Whatever. Everything started getting worse. It never occurred to Irv that for such a silly thing, he'd have to get his own lawyer. He was going to go to court himself, but his friends in business told him he had to have a formal answer to Carl's lawyer within a certain time period. He didn't know from such formalities. A lawyer should do it, I told him. He was so stubborn he almost missed the deadline, but at the last minute he hired the young son of one of his customers. The boy just passed the bar, and he was looking for work. He didn't even have an office yet.

"The boy did all the back and the forth, and the questions and the answers—each one on this blue-covered paper with all the language. I never saw so much language. Our papers told our side—that the old man left his bakery business and all his secret recipes to Carl and Irv together, and Irv was entitled to use the recipes in other places besides just that one rented building where Carl ran his father's bakery.

"Carl's papers said the recipes were part and parcel of that one bakery that was left to the boys, and when Irv left the building, he had to leave the recipes behind or else he was 'appropriating' them.

"Carl started talking real bad about Irv, too, and Irv heard about it through his customers. It was an awful time."

Anna's breathing is uneven, and I'm alarmed. I guess alarmed is too strong a word, but my guilt starts kicking in. There are times when people need to exert themselves, and this has obviously been one of those times, but there are limits. It turns out I don't have to shoulder the burden, because more than an hour has passed, and Cousin Sara walks in. *She's* alarmed.

"She looks awful," Sara says, talking to both of us, but giving me an especially accusatory look. "I knew I should have come back sooner. I see her every day and you don't," she reminds us, "and right now her color is not good."

"Oh, I'm not that bad, Sara," Anna says. She lies back, though, and lets Sara check her pulse. "What day is it today?" she asks.

"Now, Anna, you know it's Wednesday." Sara looks at us and continues to talk over Anna's head as if she weren't there. Anna starts humming "Take Me Out to the Ball Game," and Sara rolls her eyes.

What I'm seeing is Anna's rerun of "Return to Senility." I can't believe it. This lucid, with-it woman is regressing right in front of our eyes. And it doesn't seem to be an act, either.

We stay while she has her lunch, each hoping we can continue after she's finished.

She gets back in bed to drink Red Zinger tea, and we suggest that Sara might want to have some lox and bagels in the kitchen while we're still here to watch Anna. I can tell she's torn between thinking this is a great idea, and not wanting to leave us brigands alone with her Anna. The bagels win, and she stays in the kitchen.

Milt doesn't seem to have the nerve to start the conversation again, but I do. I'm just hoping the senility part of her takes off to be with Cousin Sara in the kitchen.

"How did the lawsuit between Carl and Irv come out, Anna?"

"Lawsuit?"

Uh-oh. I press on.

"I mean when the young lawyer Irv hired went to court about the secret recipes."

Anna's thinking. What she's thinking about, I don't know yet.

"There wasn't any lawsuit," she said.

"But, Mom," Milt puts in, "you said they went to court over this."

"They started it in court," she said, "but they didn't finish it. I don't know what happened to the lawsuit. It went away."

Milt looks at me as if this is hopeless. "She's forgetting again," he whispers. I'm not so sure. I make one more try.

"Dismissed? Was it dismissed?"

"Irv started brooding," she says. "Carl was always the brooder, and Irv was the good-natured one. But Irv all of a sudden wouldn't talk to me. He didn't pay any attention to his baby boy, either. He thought about those blue papers all the time.

"Then we didn't hear nothing for a while, and Irv got in a better mood. He thought maybe Carl changed his mind. He told the boy fresh from law school that he wouldn't be needing him anymore.

"We were in the store one day, and I had my back to our front show window. I wasn't looking out that window, but it didn't matter. I could tell, without looking, that bad luck was coming toward us. The man in the white suit and the Panama straw hat was back. He came in and handed Irv a new set of papers. Irv was so upset he took them with floured hands—without even wiping them on his apron. The man in the white suit said Irv wasn't allowed to open his shop anymore until everything was settled. The judge said.

"Irv got so quiet that night I got scared. He walked

around all night, brooding. In the morning, he talked. He called his baker helper and told him not to come in. Then he put the CLOSED sign in the front window.

" 'He drove me to it,' Irv said. 'I would've never done this, Anna,' he said to me. 'But now I'm driven to it.'

" 'You wouldn't go try to hurt him,' I said.

"He said, 'No. I'm not a killer or a maimer. But my brother is so stupid and empty-headed that he can't even put two and two together and figure out what I could do to him. He has no idea. He's not bright enough to figure it out.'

"That's all Irv ever said about it. All. He went out that morning and I asked him if he was going to see Carl and he said no. He was out for the whole morning, and he came back looking better. I asked and asked, but he never spoke about any of it again."

"Did Carl's store burn down or anything?" Milt asks.

"No. Nothing happened. The lawsuit went away. The man in the white suit with the Panama straw hat never came back. We opened the store the next day, too, but the man didn't come back."

"So why did you finally decide to divorce him?" Milt asks.

"Later that year he got a special girlfriend and he wouldn't give her up. Lots of women in those days looked the other way. I looked for a little while, but I wasn't going to share him with another woman. Not that way. So I divorced him."

"But the Carl thing," I say. "What happened with Carl?"

"Carl went out of business that very month, and moved Ida and his two kids to New Jersey. They opened a bakery there—what people called a sweets bakery. He didn't sell bagels. He didn't do very well, either. His customers weren't that interested in layer cakes. Ida made the layer cakes. She never was a good cook."

"Did she tell you what happened?" I ask.

"No. We never spoke again."

chapter
21

....

"Milt, do you think she told us everything?" I ask as we sit on the tailgate of his van eating our lox and bagels and watching the tide come in.

"I don't know. Grace always says my mother has secrets she'll carry to the grave, but I'm not so sure. She opened up more today than she ever has before. I do think that when people get older, they let go of lots of things they once thought it important to hold on to. Maybe she's told us all she knows."

"I guess the bottom line is that she's told us all she's going to, whatever the reason. I'm just picking at this because I'm curious. On the one hand, it's logical to me that if Irv didn't want your mother to know how he had finally made Carl give up, he would have done just what she says he did—quit talking about it and get back to business as usual. On the other hand, she appeared to be a true partner to him during all the problems with the court papers—he seems to have told her everything."

"How do we know that?" Milt says as he hands me a cold can of root beer. "They got a divorce a few months later, didn't they? And he ran around on her. We have no idea what he really let her in on. It makes more sense to me that she did tell us all she knows."

Maybe so. As I told him, it really doesn't matter, since neither of us thinks we're going to grill her more than we have already.

On the way home, we're pretty quiet. I don't know what Milt's thinking, but I'm thinking I have a lot to tell Turner when I phone him at his trial in Oklahoma. This was definitely the right thing to do today, and I can pass along all this to Nathan in New York, too. You never know what results this new information might spark.

E-mail from: Nan
To: Ruby
Subject: *Down to the Sea in Ships*

I couldn't believe you typed me that big *megillah* so late last night. If I'd had the day you did, I'd have come home and crashed. *Otoh*, I can see that you were probably too wired to sleep.

Sounds as though you have plenty to keep your little snoopy juices going for at least two months! Or two minutes, depending.

I agree you should go to other sources for the rest of the lowdown on the brothers. I still think you should have pumped Uncle Aaron more when you were in New York, even though he was more reluctant than Nathan to pursue this.

But enough about you. On the home front, I'm engaged in a game of chicken with the esteemed esquire who employs me. I know he doesn't believe I'll leave. You'll be happy to know, though, that as a result of your noodging, I did send for a copy of the LSAT sample exam and I have a lunch date with a law student I know to find out if I'd be able to do some part-time secretarial work to support myself if I were to take the plunge.

Just so you won't get too excited, though, remember these are just baby steps, and what I've always heard is that one just doesn't have the time for part-time work and a full-time law school load.

• •

E-mail from: Ruby
To: Nan
Subject: *Down to the Sea and Hips*

I'm feeling queasy today, and I think I know why. We turned the food pyramid upside down yesterday. I think the only veggie Milt and I had for the whole day was a pickle. We had bagels for breakfast, lunch, and dinner. Lox was our protein and the cream cheese was the calcium. I can't think of anything else we ate. Oh, I ate a strawberry at the apartment. So maybe it wasn't such a bad day.

On the other subject, why don't you look into a Kaplan course to prepare you for the law school admissions test? They'll probably be able to answer some of your other questions, too. With your experience, you'll be way ahead of the other applicants. I would say some encouraging things about your taking my suggestions, or at least listening, about law school. But I won't because, knowing you, I'm afraid it'll backfire on me. So for now, I'll agree with you that you're just taking baby steps, and I won't push. Too much.

I was too busy talking to you about Anna last night to mention the other topic of conversation on the way home from the coast. Milt and I started talking seriously about my buying in as his partner in the business. I know you've been concerned in the past about the bakers' hours, which, to say the least, aren't my hours. But he assured me that the production would not be my area, and there's no reason I'd have to keep the hours he does. This made it a lot easier to consider such a big step. I want to make my decision asap because of all the other things on Milt's plate right now. He can use a boost, though that's not why I'm doing this. I honestly think I'll love it, and my hours would still be my own to arrange.

More later.

chapter
22

·······················

I pull into my brand-new personalized parking space at The Hot Bagel. Milt has obviously just run out a few minutes ago and stuck up a cardboard sign with my name scrawled on it, but nevertheless, I get a kick out of it. We've waited until the late-afternoon lull to have me come down for, as he calls it, a small announcement party.

The staff is still on duty, and Grace is here, too, on her way from dropping off their youngest kid at Brownies. Milt asks us all to sit down at one of the round customer tables.

"I've asked some of you to stay for a few minutes beyond your shifts," he says, "so you won't miss out on an important announcement I'm making. I should say, an announcement that 'we're' making, because it's going to be 'we' instead of 'I' from now on. We're making a fundamental change in ownership of the bakery. Ruby Rothman is going to be my new partner. Lord help us, because we're probably going to be run by computer in the foreseeable future."

Grace claps and I laugh, but we're the only ones reacting. The UnHoly Three are sitting there openmouthed as Milt reaches under the table and pulls out a bottle of champagne. We toast in Styrofoam, but it makes no difference. I'm touched.

"Speech, speech," Milt says.

"Thanks, Gracie, for coming down, too," I say. "It means a lot. We haven't had many things to celebrate lately, and you're such a *mensch*, Milt, to put aside your own troubles to get excited about this. Stu loved you two as much as I do, and I know he's smiling down on this." It's suddenly a hard moment for me, but I recover.

"Milt, I feel honored that you wanted me as your partner, and I want to toast to many years of doing business together. I hope I can relieve some of the pressure for you and hold up my end. And to the staff, I promise that you won't be replaced by robots. It'll be a pleasure working with you." I bite my tongue on this last, but I certainly don't intend to have people fired as I make my entrance. If Milt has confidence in this group, I'm sure I can get used to them. He has his three regulars here— Bradley, Carol, and Gus. The part-time kids are in and out every semester, and I already know the ones who are currently employed.

Bradley and Carol are whispering. Finally, Carol comes out with it.

"So how come you didn't tell us, Milt? We're here every day." No congrats for me, I notice.

"Well, you heard us kidding about it a lot, so it can't be that big a surprise. We just hadn't worked out all the kinks yet. You're hearing now before everyone else."

I can see Grace is irritated, since she's not the saint Milt is. "You three have worked for us a long time," she says, "but I'm sure you know the difference between being an owner and an employee. You're all valued employees, but this is an ownership decision."

"Look," I say. "I understand that change brings uncertainty, and that can make people nervous. Just let me say that Milt's still here in full force, and we don't plan any major changes right now. Your jobs will be just as they always were."

"You should probably be getting back to work and the shift change," Milt says. Gus gets up first, and to my surprise, he comes over and shakes my hand. He looks ashen, but I appreciate the intent. Carol and Bradley, looking just as shocked, apparently decide to follow suit.

"Well, I guess I'll be calling you boss now," Bradley says with a weak attempt at a smirk. I think this is supposed to be some sort of positive gesture, so I say thanks.

Carol shakes her head, gulps something like "Me, too," and scoots into the kitchen. Milt goes in after them—whether to give some work orders or to apologize, we don't know.

"This is Milt's fault," Grace says. "For years, he's let the inmates run the asylum. This crew talks back to him all the time. They were even nasty to *me* when I filled in for him last month. Maybe you can set some limits. At home, if I weren't around to be the bad guy, our own kids would be ruling the roost."

I put this on my mental agenda for way later, but she's clearly embarrassed by my reception as new partner.

"Don't worry about it," I say. "People on a salary can be pretty single-minded. They're just worried about what might happen to their jobs."

"A hell of a way to get on your good side," she says, and I can't disagree.

The three of us celebrate again in a more pleasant atmosphere by having a good dinner together at the new Asian restaurant down the street. I need to finish early so I can go to one of the umpteen committee meetings at Essie Sue's house. The bakery's closed now, but Milt and Grace drop me off there after dinner to get my car, and they send me off with waves good-bye. I'm thinking about our new venture as I head for Essie Sue's house in the hills.

It's hot outside, but the evening air is thick with honey-suckle, so I forgo air conditioning for an open window. It's fun to drive in these neighborhoods—so steep that I need a lower gear to climb the hills. There's no traffic at all, and I'm going up, up, and up as I circle around the top of Bold Mountain. It's a little creepy on these winding roads at night, and the car might feel safer with the windows up, but I'm enjoying the air too much. The university radio station has Celtic folksingers on—not usually my cup of tea, but these voices are positively hypnotic. They're right at home in these woods—Pan-like when they hit the high registers.

So the truth is, I'm procrastinating. I'd be going even more slowly if I weren't dealing with the steady push of the gas pedal up these roads. The lights are going on one by one in the valley, some so far away they look like the fireflies that are flickering in these woods. I should use my cell phone to call and tell them I'm running a little late, but I refuse to ruin this marvelous drive by letting Essie Sue's staccato burst through the night air at me. The phone's too expensive to use, anyway. I only got it because I was logging so many miles schlepping to my work sites. Now that I'll be spending equal time at the bakery, I'm going to unsubscribe.

I realize tonight's a milestone of sorts. I'm convinced the bakery partnership is a good investment for me, but I'm not doing it just for the financial security it can offer down the line. I need to be back in touch with human beings. I've bounced around for almost two years now, supporting myself with the computer consulting but not feeling really soul fed. Working with things instead of people after Stu died was exactly what I needed. It helped me regain my equilibrium without costing me too much in the way of emotional currency.

Some healing must have been going on, because I find myself moving more easily through my life since the New York trip. I could never have made a visit to see the Rothmans even a few months ago—too many painful reminders. But whatever happened there worked. I came back ready to have my feet go forward, even though my head might not be there yet.

The Hot Bagel is a good first step. I like being part of a place where people gather to enjoy themselves, where I'll hear all the news and the schmooze, with a partner who'll allow me some room. The Temple's still a big part of me, which is why I suppose I allow myself to keep sparring with the likes of Essie Sue and Kevin.

The connection there for me is worth the effort—if the effort doesn't overwhelm me.

As I head toward Essie Sue's house on the other side of Bold Mountain, I shudder to think what surprises she's got planned for tonight's meeting. My foot has a cramp in it from the constant pressing down on the accelerator, and I'm in a hurry now to be there and have this over with. The closer I get to the mountaintop, the less I'm enjoying the night and the view—though the lights are gorgeous up this high.

The slope is gentle at first as I begin the descent to Essie Sue's house in the valley. The road curves almost horizontally for a while, and I'm relieved to take my foot off the gas pedal and coast for a bit. I bet I'd be a good race-car driver—I like negotiating turns.

Braking is automatic for me. So when the grade steepens, I suppose I put my foot on the brake pedal, although I don't think consciously about it because I'm still being lulled by the trill of the Celtic wood nymphs.

For a second I think I'm still coasting. I must be coasting because the wheel feels loose the way it does when there's no drag on the car. I can't feel that secure heaviness the brakes bring. In another second, it's all looseness and emptiness as I push on the brake pedal and get nothing. Oh God—what are you supposed to do? Throw it in neutral? No, that's snow and ice. Throw it in low gear.

I throw it in low gear. It doesn't help much. I can't see outside the perimeter of the headlights, so I don't know how steep the grade is on the inside curve of the road. If I swerve off the road toward the woods, I can't tell if the car would fall down into blackness or not. The outside curve, the curve with the view, I don't let myself even think about. I'm race-car driving, trying to steer and keep the car on the narrow road.

The car's going faster and faster and I have to do something, so I swerve to the right and bump and tumble into the blackness of the woods. I'm most scared that the car will fall down and down into nowhere. It keeps heading rightward, and I can feel it turning over on its right side, but there is ground there, not just the blackness. I feel the wheels bounce at the same time the windshield hits a tree. I'm stopped.

I lie there, still buckled in, for what seems a very long time, just getting my bearings. My side of the car is now the top, and my window is facing upward toward the night sky. I feel for my own arms and legs like a mother inspecting a newborn's fingers and toes. I'm all there. My head wasn't impacted, probably because we—I seem to be calling the car and me "we"—fell on our side before we hit the tree. My air bag, which I never trusted anyway, has not opened, and if it had, it probably would have given me a heart attack.

Needless to say, if the car had turned over on the driver's side, I wouldn't be up in the air like this trying to open the left car door. I would have been crushed like the seat below me seems to be. And if I had waited much longer to swerve off the road, I'd have lost control of the car and gone careening off the mountain. Thank you, God.

I feel no pain whatever. I know from my many childhood horseback riding accidents that if you're in shock, the pain comes a few minutes later—unless you've broken something. I don't think I've broken anything.

When I was riding bareback—to my parents' consternation—and falling a lot, I learned the drill, and I could tell immediately if something was broken. I also learned to get myself moving fast—there were bulls in some of those riding pastures.

I don't want to think about any gasoline problems, either. I just need to hurry. The door's stuck, but the window's wide open and my side of the car seems intact. I'm stuck myself, though—I can't seem to move. Oh— the seat belt. The damn thing won't unbuckle. I'm pushing on the square button when I realize that the seat belt is the only thing keeping me from sinking down sideways toward the crushed glass of the passenger window. Suddenly, everything hurts when I try to get my legs out from below the steering wheel. So much for my brief period of numbness.

I can't let myself worry about the pain—I'm too scared of the gasoline fumes I'm smelling.

Okay, you can do this, Ruby. It would help if my life were flashing in front of me, but it isn't. So much for that myth. In fact, I have to force myself to flash on anything from the past that might help get me out of here. The memories are not working. I can only recall that a couple of years ago I thought our plane was going to crash on the way home from California. They'd just served us one of those Mexicali Chicken airline dinners, and I remember thinking to myself—you mean *that* was my last meal?

I do remember something from much further back, though, when I was nine or ten. In fact, if I push it, I can even see that it was a similar situation. Kind of. My boyfriend and I had wedged ourselves up under his house. I don't even want to think why. It was a tight space, and I was stuck on my side. We thought we smelled gas that time, too, and I panicked. He got out but couldn't pull me free. I remember his telling me to find something to push off, and I pushed my feet against a pier to slide out where he could reach me.

I need to get leverage. I brace one hand against the passenger seat before I try to unbuckle again, so I won't slip toward the broken window near the ground. The buckle unpops, thank you, God, and I plant my right foot on the divider thing between the front seats where you're not supposed to keep the talking book tapes in the summer time. It works—I have enough leverage to pull my other leg up into a semicrouch, and then to use both arms to hoist myself up through the driver's window to the outside. The car's on its side, which means I'm sitting on top of the whole mess with my feet dangling.

When I jump the short distance to the ground, everything hurts, indiscriminately. I hope I can run, because I want to get some distance from the car. Fast. Just as I'm gearing up to face the pain that is now unavoidable, I remember the cell phone. I've gotta grab it, or I'll be here half the night. And in case I've really hurt something, at least I can get some emergency medical attention.

I do a quick balance sheet. Do I risk going back to the car for the phone and maybe get myself blown up, or do I run a safe distance, pronto? My mind is made up by something with teeth that rushes by me in the woods. It's not big, and it's probably more scared of me than I am of it. Yeah, that's what they all say. I'm making a grab for the cell phone.

I grit my teeth and climb up the toppled car far enough to reach in the open window. I definitely don't want to fall back in there, so I hold on tight to the side mirror, which is all I can find to clutch. I've always wanted longer arms—never more so than now. I reach blindly and just when my fingers touch the phone, something furry and not nice rubs against my arm. I get goosebumps. Let's just say that the words animal, night, and woods have never been a favorite combination of mine, not even in ghost stories. I squeeze my hand around the cell phone, jump, and run.

At a safe distance (I have no idea what a safe distance might be, and I have no intention of venturing too far from the road) I sit down in the dirt. I'm now trembling, but I manage the 911. Now all I have to do is speak into the phone. Aloud, that is. I thought this would be the easy part, but it's not. My voice isn't doing what it's supposed to do. Fortunately, the operator is trained to be patient. At last, my tax dollars have gone for something worthwhile.

I tell her I'm on the down side of Bold Mountain Road. She reminds me Bold Mountain Road has two down sides, depending on which way you're coming down the mountain. I'm not thinking too well, and she suggests I give her the address of where I started from and where I was headed. We work it out. I ask her if she'd mind staying on the phone, although what she could do if something attacked me or the car blew up, I don't know. At least I'd have a witness.

The 911 lady's company would be nice except for the

fact I can no longer hold the phone to my ear. I drop it on the ground in front of me and just sit and stare at it, hurting all over and crying because I've forgotten to get the flashlight from the glove compartment. That's okay, though, because it has no batteries in it. I went into my garage one night and took them out to use in my portable cream whipper that came as a bonus for joining the Chocolate Cooking Club. I'm such a jerk. The thing wouldn't whip shit.

chapter
23

· ·

I must have driven deeper into the woods than I thought, since it's totally black out here. I know I'm not *that* far from the road, but I just hope they can find me. I think I'm a safe distance from the car, and I don't smell any fumes. Chances are good the car won't blow up. My, I do sound like an expert.

I hear rustling, and that says snakes to me. Just don't let it be a snake. I decide I'd better pick up the phone for some courage. My lady is named Marie, and I'm thankful for her.

"How can they find me if there's no light?" I ask her.

"They have lights," she assures me, "and this isn't that long a stretch of road." I feel better.

"Do you know if they've started already?"

Marie assures me they have.

I'm either sitting on wet leaves or I've wet my pants—I don't know which, Maybe both. I hope this doesn't attract snakes. I've never been more scared in my life. I hate snakes.

Marie tells me to try to think of something to take my mind off where I am. This is not easy. It does occur to me that this is a pretty great excuse not to go to the meeting.

Marie asks me if I want her to call anyone who might be expecting me, and I tell her no. All I need is Rabbi Kevin hiking out here to make a sick call. Although maybe they could help search. I'm sure Essie Sue's never looked for something she couldn't find. No, there's no need for a search. Yet. They'll just think I blew off the meeting. Now I'm really glad I didn't call from the car to say I'd be late. Let 'em talk about me. Let 'em eat cake. Let 'em eat Essie Sue's kiwi tarts. I'm definitely losing it out here. Why didn't I keep that little flashlight Billy Frankenmeyer made for me on a lanyard at camp? He said I'd never know when I'd need it. Ha. *If* the batteries were in it.

If I can just keep my mind off all the serious questions that are popping up in my brain about this accident, maybe I can get through this. I tell Marie I was a Girl Scout. She seems unimpressed. I tell her I think I should try to go out on the road and wave them down. She tells me to stay put. I ask her if she's ever talked anyone through delivering a baby. She says yes. It suddenly becomes very important to me that Marie not think that I'm drunk. She says nobody who talks this fast could possibly be drunk. I'm just nervous, she says. Nervous? Try scared shitless. No, not exactly shitless, apparently.

Cars. I hear cars. I expect to hear sirens, but there aren't any. I hear garbage truck–like noises, engines going very slowly. Suddenly, huge searchlights are combing the woods. I try to yell "Over here," but it doesn't sound like I remember from the movies. Marie says not to exhaust myself—she'll tell them I see the lights. Oh. I get it. She's talking to them at the same time she's talking to me. Why didn't she tell me that? She's probably advising them to bring a net.

I relax now that I'm sure they won't pass me by and move down the highway. Next thing I know, the truck stops and they're shining lights on me. I'm telling two big, strong, wonderful women saviors that I don't need a stretcher. I can walk. Well, sort of. I'm glad they're strong, because they're having to cope with the fact that I not only have rubber legs, but that I'm wailing like the sirens that never materialized.

I still have Marie on the phone. Once I'm safe in the van and lying on a cot, my brain unscrambles. Whether I like it or not, I'm going to have to let some very ugly thoughts in, and I don't have the luxury of letting hysteria get in the way. I'm all business.

"Marie, I want you to listen very carefully. Do not let a regular towing service come and haul this car away. I don't want the car tampered with until the police can examine it. The brakes gave way completely when I began to come down the other side of the mountain. I'm sure the lines were cut. And just in case you think I'm the same nut you've been so lovingly taking care of all night, trust me. I'm sane now. I have good reasons to think this wasn't an accidental brake failure."

"I'm with you," she says. "And all this is being recorded, in case your nerves get the best of you once you get to the hospital. It happens, you know."

"The hospital? I don't think I need to go to the hospital."

"Maybe it'll just be the emergency room, to make sure," she soothes me. "It's standard procedure."

"Okay, if you're sure it's standard procedure," I say stupidly. I think I'm all business only part of the time.

"And I don't want them knocking me out with any pills," I say, "before I speak with Lieutenant Lundy at the police department. Make them call him at home if he's off duty. He knows me. Will you promise, Marie? If I don't speak to him now, I'm afraid this whole thing could get deep-sixed. And I don't think I could bear to have to explain to someone else what he already knows."

I'm sobbing again now.

"Ruby, save your energy," Marie says. "I promise you I'll have this Lundy meet you at the hospital. If he's home, that is, or on duty."

"Thanks" is all I can muster.

My two angels of mercy have been listening, and come through for me again. They tell the driver to put the siren on.

I lose track of time for a while. One of the angels tells me I dozed off, but I doubt it. I do know that I don't offer to walk into the hospital—they don't ask, and I just let them carry me in on the gurney. I'm too tired to care.

I'm lying in one of those little curtained cubicles trying to decide which was worse—the moment I swerved into the woods or the moment I heard the snakes—when Lieutenant Lundy walks in. I can't believe he got here so fast, but now I'm not sure I want to see him. I'm regretting that instant of clarity in the ambulance when I realized this wasn't an accident.

"Hi," I say wanly. "I'm not feeling well enough to deal with all this now. I'm really grateful you came and all that . . ."

"Oh no you don't—" he says. "You got me out of a poker game in my apartment—a game I was winning, I might add."

I can see he's trying to lighten me up, but I'm having none of it. "No, really. I apologize, but can we make it another day? I haven't even been examined yet. I might have a concussion, and anything I say might be off."

"I'll take my chances. Marie told me she was really impressed with your sense of urgency about preserving the evidence from the accident." Lundy looks cute. I don't even know his first name, but I've seen him in the bakery forever. He's wearing khaki shorts and sandals and a rather formal-looking short-sleeved white dress shirt—probably from his workday. He's slight and vulnerable-looking, but his eyes are sharp. I liked the way he listened when I gave him the report of my near-miss incident on Village Street.

He perches on his rolling stool. "People forget things after a day," he says. "Even after a few hours. Especially if they're personally involved. There's something else working against us, too. It's human nature not to want to believe you might have enemies. Trust me. This is my business. Get this out now and you won't have to go through it later. You'll love it that you spilled it all on *my* head so it can be my worry."

I couldn't have said it better myself, and I'm an ace

number one persuader. I'm also extremely hardheaded if someone approaches me with the wrong logic. This guy thinks like I do—especially the part about loving it later—that's original, and tailor-made for my type. If he'd told me to go through this to get justice, I'd have figured I could do that when I felt better.

So we go through every little boring detail. I give him my evening minute by minute. In addition, he listens to all my practical theories about Milt's being framed, my wilder theories about some family involvement through the years and across the miles, a recitation of everything I know about Gus, Bradley, Carol, and yes, even Essie Sue.

"And none of this," I say, "explains in the slightest why someone would want *me* dead or hurt. Maybe Marla's murderer thinks I'm getting too close, but close to what? The truth is that I don't know any more than you do. Except that you all think Milt did it, and I know he didn't."

"Milt had every opportunity to do it," Lundy says. "And you have to keep remembering what we don't know. We don't even know yet if your brakes were tampered with. We don't know if there's any connection at all with the hit-and-run. If you remember, you also talked to me earlier about some as yet unproven connection between Rabbi Rothman's death and all of this. I need your help in exploring some of these avenues."

"Why? If the juggernaut is moving toward Milt," I say, "and my gut, or bias, or whatever you want to call it, leaves me unable to consider at all that he's guilty, then how can I help the police?"

"You're saying two things," he says. "You're saying

'you,' and you're saying 'the police.' We have a case against your friend. That's one level. But the investigation into these matters is not closed. That's another level. And my own efforts as an individual police officer might sometimes be different from the police position. I'm trusted, and I have a certain amount of leeway at my level. Not a lot, but some."

"So? Are you saying you're open to the possibility that Milt, who's someone you've known in the bakery for a lot of years, too, I might add, might not have done it?"

"I'm admitting it's a complex case. As you know, we don't have to prove motive, and as of now, we can't. Means and opportunity we've got plenty of. But I've always been interested in a possible tie-in between the threats made to your husband to stay away from Milt and the situation we have now, with Milt being . . ."

"Framed for murder?"

"Quit putting words in my mouth. Geez, I'd hate to put *you* on the stand."

"Oh, I'll get myself on there, one way or the other."

"I'm sure you will." He changes the subject. "I knew your husband, too, you know."

"No, I didn't know that. I'm glad."

"He was a lovely man, Mrs. Rothman. And I don't use that word too often."

"Not a guy word. He was a lovely man. Thanks."

I'm about to cry again when what looks like a twelve-year-old boy comes in and wants to examine me. What the hell—he's got a white coat, and I'm not that sick, anyhow, if you don't count pain in every fiber inside competing with fire ant welts on every inch outside. I guess Junior here can find out if I have any snakebites.

"Sorry about the poker game," I say to Lundy. "And you were right. I am very glad I unloaded this on you. You helped me."

"I hate to admit this," he says to both of us, "but one of the reasons I came down here right away was that I knew we'd have a lot of interview time before the emergency staff would be free to examine you. A long, quiet time with a witness is like gold to me in an investigation."

"Two things—" I say to him. "Do they let you use a first name besides Lieutenant? Mine's Ruby. And second—seriously, did I manage to get across that I'm scared?"

"Paul. Yeah, I got the message, Ruby. It came through the feisty part that you're scared."

"Thanks, Paul."

"And what's *your* name?" I ask the doctor. Always get their name.

chapter
24

....

E-mail from: Ruby
To: Nan
Subject: *I Almost Hate to Tell You This*

First of all, I'm home and okay. I'm prepared for the fact that you're going to get hysterical, Nan, but I have to ask you to hold it in. *Please* don't pick up the phone when you get this—my voice is shaky and I can't deal with anything too face-to-face. I'm doing e-mail because I wanted to touch base with you in case you don't hear from me for a few days, and the medium happens to be just fine for my message. Just don't give me any advice right now.

I'm in bed with Oy Vay at my feet, and I can hardly move a muscle. I want to write a note before I take the Tylenol 3 they gave me and crash.

I ran my car off the road tonight and it turned over on its side. Fortunately, the driver's side was up and I climbed out before anything bad could happen. Nothing exploded. I used my cell phone—yeah, the one I was getting ready to cancel—to call the emergency and they came pretty fast. I was checked out at the hospital just in case, and nothing was wrong with me. I definitely didn't bang my head, so don't worry about a concussion. This is not serious enough to call Joshie tonight, btw— I'll tell him later.

Paul Lundy, the cop I made the first report to, came and talked to me. He wants to examine the car. Don't worry about this ahead of time—something like this could take weeks to investigate. I think I've convinced him to at least look into other possibilities. We'll see.

I'm fine. And just to lighten things up here—I did get out of a boring meeting.

Since it's three in the morning already, part of me wants to turn off my phone so I can sleep late. I guess I'd better keep the lines open in case Paul gets back to me in a hurry. *Oy*—I forgot to tell him not to talk to Milt before I do.

I'm dreaming that I'm trapped inside the glass casing of an old grandfather clock, and the pendulum is hitting my head at the stroke of midnight with twelve gigantic gongs. The gongs reverberate—they won't go away. I'm trying to rouse myself but it's not working. Oy Vay is licking my ear and running in and out of the room. Those gongs—I can't stand it. I sit up in bed and realize it's the doorbell—an amazingly loud and insistent door-bell whose ring couldn't possibly be mine. I could never put up with a doorbell that made that much noise. Nevertheless, it seems to be my doorbell. Oy Vay is scratching at the door running back to lick me then going into the whole routine all over again. Midday light is streaming in—could I have slept until noon?

I run downstairs mindlessly in the direction of the bell—anything to shut out those gongs. As I throw the front door open, I suddenly realize I'm wearing the Wonder Woman long tee shirt—the one that shrunk years ago but that I can't give up. It's made of a soft, light gray cotton that feels like a security blanket. About a foot too short at this point, it covers everything, but barely.

Yep, I'm still nightmaring. My worst nightmare. Essie Sue, in a pale pink linen suit and white strap heels, looks as if she's dressed for the annual Women's Guild fashion show. Yikes, she *is* dressed for the fashion show. Rabbi Kapstein is two steps behind her, in gray pinstripes and new wing tips. Since there was no other rabbi's wife around, I was supposed to give the invocation at the fashion show today. Invoking for a fashion show takes imagination, trust me.

It's a standoff. We all stare at one another, and I do one of those half dips, half curtsies that's supposed to make the hem of the tee shirt longer, but only succeeds in directing all eyes below my waistline. I back up geisha-girl fashion with my hands crossed in front of me, and to my horror, this is construed as an invitation to follow me inside. I should have tried to slam the door—not that it would have worked. They don't make a door that can slam on Essie Sue against her wishes. The rabbi kicks it shut with the back of his foot—even in my drugged-out fog, I can see this is a hostile gesture. She must be on the warpath if he's dared to innovate.

"Where were you last night?" she starts in. "You could have at least had the courtesy to call. And why aren't you dressed for the luncheon?"

Kevin pipes in. "Last night we created some very important fund-raising forms to ease the committee's work, and you missed the explanation. Now you won't know . . ."

"I told you I wasn't doing the fund-raising part. I'm supposed to help you with the installation."

I'm still backing up, and as I back into my rocking chair and fall into it, I'm momentarily jolted out of my fog. Is this surreal, or is this surreal? My life could be in danger, I'm covered with bruises and bites from head to foot, and I'm arguing with Kevin about his installation.

I let them rant while I try to push the fog back. Kevin's shielding his face with his hand as if to protect himself from any frontal nudity that might suddenly emerge. Essie Sue's deciding where she can safely sit without dirtying the pink linen, and Oy Vay is happily rubbing against both of them.

The doorbell rings again, and it sounds benign compared to the ruckus going on.

It's Paul. I'm so grateful I almost kiss his feet.

"What are you doing out of bed?"

"Answering the door for you and entertaining friends."

"Touché."

He's obviously pretending not to notice the knotted, uncombed hair, the red welts from hell, or the very alluring sleepwear. Then again, he saw me last night when I was worse.

"Paul, help me out. I got jolted out of bed a minute ago, and I'm not awake yet. The woman in the living room is the one whose house I was heading to last night when I ran off the road. That's the new rabbi with her. Could you please go into the room, introduce yourself, and explain to them why I missed the meeting? If you can get them to leave, that's even better, but don't count on it. I've got to get dressed."

"I'll only help you out if you go get back in bed. Then I've got to talk to you."

"Fair enough. I'm feeling woozy, anyway."

I try to run upstairs to the bedroom, but it's more like a Frankenstein lurch. I'm wondering if police action will excuse me from the invocation.

No such luck. Paul comes into the room with the two of them. "I couldn't persuade them to come back later," he says. "Sorry."

"Better men than you have tried," I say.

Actually, I'd rather get it over with now than later. They're hovering over my bed before I know what hit me.

"You should have called me from the car phone to help," Essie Sue says, "but we won't go into that now. I'm just glad you didn't break anything. This is such an important time of year." She sits on my bed with the best of intentions, I'm sure, but I can only take so much of her brand of comfort today. In case she's gonna take my hands, I hide them preemptively under the covers. She definitely wouldn't like what scrambling for my life did to my fingernails.

"I can't understand why I wasn't notified to make a hospital call," Kevin says, looking at me as if it must be my fault. "Did you fill out 'Jewish' on the admission form?"

"No," I say, falling back on the pillows. "It wasn't the first thing on my mind."

"Rabbi, she was brought in to the emergency room, and she didn't fill out any forms," Paul lies. When are there not forms? You could be dying and they'd hand you a form to get preapproved. Still, Kevin seems pacified.

"Looking at you objectively," Essie Sue tells me, "I don't think we could do a successful makeup job so that you'd pass at the fashion show."

"Pass for what?"

Ignoring that, she mercifully makes a judgment that I'm a lost cause for now. Not to mention what I might invoke once I got behind the mike at the head table. The woman's no dummy.

"We're going to be late," she says to Kevin, and heads out the door. Her departures, like her phone exits, are unmarked. I'm relieved and breathing easily again, when she sticks her head back in.

"Do you have a pretty, *clean* bed jacket, dear? Better put it on. After I make my announcement at the luncheon, there'll be lots of goodies headed your way."

Paul lets them out. I pretend to be asleep when he gets back. I didn't like the sound of his voice when he said he wanted to talk to me. I think I'd prefer to wimp it out for another day or so before hearing anything bad.

"Sorry," he says, "but what I have to tell you can't wait."

I'm awake. "The brake lines were cut, right?" Saying it before he does means I don't have to hear it coming out of his mouth. This is one of those Rubyish reactions that gets me absolutely nowhere. But that hasn't stopped me from doing it most of my life.

"Yeah, the lines were cut."

"I haven't talked to Milt," I say. "He'll be mad at me for not calling him right away."

"So what are you thinking?" He's not buying the digression. Only it wasn't totally a digression. Milt needs to be told, and I'm dreading it because he'll care so much.

"I'm thinking that it's probably one of those idiots who work for Milt," I say.

"There's no proof of that." It's the policeman speaking now. "The place was closed shortly after you left, and it was dark when you came back. Anyone could have been in that alley."

"How do you know when the place was closed?"

"Because I already spoke to Milt. I asked him to give you a whole day before he called or came over. I thought you needed the rest. Who knew you'd have company before I even got here?"

"It's the curse of the house," I say. "So what happens now?"

"We're reinterviewing everybody. I reviewed with the higher-ups the two attempts on your life and the phone calls made to your husband before his death warning him to stay away from Milt. The combination of those events at least warrants a search for some tie-in between your family and Milt and the bakery. There are just too many weird coincidences here."

"I'm sure the higher-ups were thrilled," I say.

"Don't do that. We're not your enemy."

I nod, but he's not finished. "You read too many mysteries. Believe it or not, we're not panting to carry forward a bad case."

"So this accident of mine is going to slow things up?"

"Definitely. My problem is that I just don't know what to do about your safety. I wish we could keep you in the house for a couple of weeks, but that's probably fantasy."

"Two days for sure. But not two weeks. On the other hand, I'm not a fool, Paul. I can try to have someone with me when I go out. And it wouldn't hurt me physically to be homebound for a while. Within reason."

"I'm still thinking about it. Maybe your son could come."

"No, his courses start soon."

"Maybe you could take a trip."

"I already took a trip."

"What, then?"

"Let me think about it. If someone wants me to stay away from the bakery, maybe I should do just that. Maybe Milt and I ought to stage a falling out and see what happens."

chapter
25

....

E-mail from: Ruby
To: Nan
Subject: *The Dough Thickens*

I really enjoyed your phone call last night, hon. I'm glad you waited for me to break out of my stupor—believe me, I would not have been a fount of information. I know you were worried. Joshie wanted to come home and take care of me, but I managed to convince him I was okay. I couldn't bring myself to tell him that this was more than an accident, though. I mean, what could he do except worry? I keep hoping that when I do have to tell him, I'll have a bead on why this is happening.

Nothing could have cheered me more than hearing you're going to study for the LSAT. Yeah, you're going to fail and all that—I've heard it before. Let's just take one thing at a time. First, the test, then applying to law school, then getting in. Okay? I'm glad you can take the

Kaplan after work so you can hold the job as a fail-safe. Once you get admitted, I'm betting Burke will be desperate to have you work part-time when you get settled in your classes.

Paul thinks the falling out with Milt idea is a stroke of genius. I'm having second thoughts about it because I wanted to spend even more time down there getting to really know the employees. There are some part-time people I've never even met. The police want me to stay out of it, of course, while they do background checks on everyone. Milt and I have to get together on our story. My guess is that he'll just let it drop in the bakery that we're having some problems and have postponed our negotiations. The partnership was supposed to have been a done deal, but actually, it was only at the handshake stage. We were going to ask Turner Goldman to draw up papers for us, but we'd postponed that.

I'm healing fast—it was only bruises and bites, anyway. I'm very lucky. The greatest incentive for feeling better in a hurry is that I'll avoid a lot of company. Of course, Paul didn't tell Essie Sue that my accident wasn't an accident, but she apparently made a big *megillah* out of it at the fashion show. Now everyone thinks I'm maimed for life, I guess. Kevin invoked for my recovery— *oy*. I've had calls from old friends, too, and I appreciated them, but enough is enough.

I'm renting a car until mine is fixed. The right side was the worst—the side that rolled over on the ground in the woods. It's definitely fixable—mainly, the doors have to be replaced or hammered out—whichever is cheaper, and they have to replace the seats.

On the Milt front, I filled Joshie in on our visit to Aransas with Milt's mom, Anna Aboud, and he's going to tell Cousin Nathan all about it. Nathan, if you remember, touched base with Carl Sebran's widow at her bakery in New Jersey. We figure Nathan will have an opening to get in another conversation with her by telling her he has news of brother Irv's ex-wife Anna.

Paul thought it would be a good idea if I concentrated on my consulting work and the temple activities for now. He thinks it'll keep me out of trouble. Believe me, I'm not looking for more trouble—it just seems to find me.

Because I've missed more of the planning for the big do at temple, I'm being taken out to dinner tonight by Essie Sue and her husband Hal for a fill-in session. Thank goodness for Hal—he's a buffer.

More later.

Essie Sue and Hal are on time at the stroke of seven. She asked earlier where I'd like to eat and I suggested a little Mexican place I like downtown, so we're having Chinese. I'm in pants, she's in a dress—the new "tubular" look, she says. I don't know from tubular. From her outfit, I'm figuring we're headed to one of the upscale Chinese in the Silicon Valley part of Austin—condo city, I call it.

"Ruby, dear, you really ought to learn to dress for any eventuality," she tells me, "like I do."

"Yeah," I say. I'm all out of retorts, having spent a half hour just getting my clothes on over the bruises. On the other hand, it's good to get out of the house. I haven't felt like cooking, and I've OD'd on the lemon squares and brownies that poured in after the fashion show announcement. I've been avoiding grocery shopping, too, so today's lunch was leftovers, and I do mean anything that was left, which turned out to be a can of artichoke hearts and some peanut brittle. The peanut brittle's the bottom of the barrel from the fashion show crowd.

I've been here before. This Chinese place has changed its decor from gilt and lacquer to mirrors and glass, and is now calling itself Asian. The menu hasn't changed, I notice. Hal orders a bourbon along with his wonton soup, and I consider doing the same, but think better of it. It wouldn't go down well with the pain pills, and who knows what I might volunteer for by the end of the evening. On the other hand, it might have made the time pass a lot more pleasantly.

"The rabbi was going to join us for dessert," Essie Sue says. I knew it. Just in time to drive me home, I'll bet. "I said *was*," she tells me. "He had to pay a condolence call." Suddenly the present company goes up a notch. I'm now actually content, thinking of what could have been.

I concentrate on my soup—hot-and-sour. I've dealt with Essie Sue for so many years I can do it from memory, but Kevin is different. He gives me the creeps, in a Uriah Heep-ish sort of way.

I soon discover that Essie Sue has an agenda in Kevin's absence, so relaxation is out the window.

She wastes no time with amenities.

"Ruby, it's simply not proper for the rabbi to be a single man at the fund-raising ball."

"But he is a single man."

Hal snorts into his bourbon and branch—a snort only

I can hear. Essie Sue is much too engrossed to notice. He signals for another drink.

"The rabbi admires you very much, you know. He's shy, though. He wanted me to pave the way."

I'm dumb. Moving me is going to be like dragging a buffalo, and she's going to have to do all the work herself.

"What could be more appropriate than the two of you coming to the ball together? You have no one and he has no one."

"What a lovely sentiment. Just calculated to make me putty in your hands."

Hal shoves over the bourbon, but I pass, even though the pain pills have probably been absorbed already in the hot-and-sour soup.

Essie Sue retracts. "That's possibly a little blunt, but you already know everyone who's coming. What difference could it make? There's no one else you'd be remotely interested in—I've checked the list."

"What makes you think I'd be 'remotely interested' in the rabbi?" She's right about the list, of course, but I wouldn't give her the satisfaction.

"What's wrong with him?"

Hal and I look at each other. "Your court," he says.

"Let me not count the ways. He's several years younger than I am, for one thing."

"What do a few years mean?"

Obviously, an objective answer isn't going to do it. "Suffice it to say he's not my type."

"How can you say that? You were married to one for years."

"There are rabbis and there are rabbis," I say. "Or do

you think I'm lusting for the whole generic group?"

"Forget lust." Easy for her to say. "Why waste all you've learned about being a rabbi's wife? This would be nothing for you. You could do it with the back of your hand."

"Do what with the back of my hand?"

She takes another tack. "He makes a very nice living."

"No."

"I thought this was just supposed to be a date, not an engagement," Hal says.

"It's about time you spoke up," I say.

"I'm sure we can work this out. Maybe another time." She's temporarily retreating. I take the stalemate as an opportunity to promote an agenda of my own.

"Let's talk about my accident," I say.

"But, darling, this dinner was supposed to make you forget about the accident."

"I appreciate that, but I need to talk to you about something that can help both of us. Can I trust you both to keep a confidence?" Paul and I have talked about this, and it's worth the gamble to turn Essie Sue's thoughts about Marla's murder in a different direction.

"About what?"

I tell them my brakes were cut, and that Milt was having dinner with me and couldn't possibly have done it. That I think my search for another more likely suspect has deeply disturbed the real killer, and that he or she is now after me. I don't mention Stu's hit-and-run being tied in—somehow I can see Essie Sue keeping quiet about my accident, but not about his. Besides, the evidence about Stu is far more speculative at this point.

She and Hal both seem stunned. I put it to her as bluntly as I can.

"Look, as I've said to you before—this is your sister we're talking about. I know you've never liked Milt, and I know he's the prime suspect. But some of the police are now rethinking this case. Surely you don't want Marla's killer out there for the duration while Milt goes to prison."

"*Oy*, Ruby, why in the world didn't you stay out of this? You've always been too inquisitive for your own good. Now you're putting your life in danger. Let the police do their work."

Hal chimes in. "For once, she's right, Ruby. I'm afraid for you."

"I'm afraid, too, but now I have more reason than ever to stay focused on this case. Knowledge is power—I really believe that. If you want to help me, then give up this one-track idea about Milt, and brainstorm for me and with me. For Marla's sake. I'll promise to stay in the background. Believe me, I'm not trying to get myself killed."

Hal looks really troubled, and I'm sorry I've upset him. "I've tried to get Essie Sue to consider some other possibilities," he says, "but her mind's closed."

This I truly don't understand, even knowing her personality. Is there something she's afraid to tell the police?

"So why can't you open your mind, Essie Sue? You're a bright woman. You can see there's more to this. I'm asking for your help."

"I still don't believe you should be sticking your nose

into this, Ruby. Maybe Milt had someone cut the brakes for him. Did you ever think of that?"

"I'm sure someone at the police station has thought of that—they're checking all possibilities."

Hal looks at me. "Ruby, I agree with you that we should look in all directions. But how can you be so absolutely certain Milt *didn't* do it?"

"I can't give you proof, Hal. I can only give you my gut instincts, built on years and years of trust."

"So you could be wrong?"

"Anybody could be wrong about anything, Hal. I'd just stake my life otherwise."

"That's what you're doing," Essie Sue says, "staking your life."

"If you're so concerned about me, then promise me you'll have a talk with Lieutenant Lundy. You met him at my house."

"Why? The police have talked with me already."

"Lundy's in charge of my case, Essie Sue. He could use any information about Marla that you may have forgotten or thought was unimportant, since he thinks the two cases are linked."

"They think that, for sure?"

"Yes. That's why I'm confiding in you."

Hal looks at her. "Say yes," he tells her.

She still looks hesitant, but she comes through. "All right. I'll talk to Lundy if I remember anything that could be helpful."

I'm feeling so grateful I give Essie Sue a real hug when they take me home from dinner—not the fake kissie-kissie routine we usually dance to. "I owe you one," I tell her.

"No you don't," she says as she waves good-bye. "We're even. You'll be the rabbi's date for the fund-raising ball."

chapter
26

....

I'm trying to get out of the house for a morning ap-
pointment with Jack's Car Rental—not always my favorite client, but they came through for me after the
accident and gave me a good deal. It's a local outfit, so
they can set their own prices. I finally got my own car
back yesterday, and it looks almost as good as new. The
doors and seats on the passenger side were replaced and
the other dents were hammered out and painted. The
engine's still zippy—I hope nothing shows up later.

Jack's Car Rental wants a Web page. Everybody
wants a Web page. My past work for them just involved
keeping their computers up and running—tracking in-
ventory and making sure the computerized phone system
worked properly. Now, they don't just want a Web page,
they want a jazzy, with-it Web page, and they want it
on the cheap. I've told them I'm not a graphic designer.

Some of these Web pages can be a crock, if you ask
me. The cheap ones look no better than an ad in the

yellow pages, and the more effective ones can be a really big deal. They're expensive to maintain and require a lot of labor-intensive support. Half my clients don't even know what they want when they talk Web site—they've just been told it's something they have to have.

The phone's been ringing all morning. Milt had Grace call from home to tell me he'd casually mentioned to the help that our partnership was on hold for a while—that we'd had some disagreements. Maybe even a rift in our friendship. Grace hinted that the staff didn't look too sorrowful at the news—guess I won't win any popularity contests down there. They'd obviously rather keep the status quo. Grace and Milt offered to have me stay at their house for safety—which would, of course, obviate all we're trying to achieve at the bakery, but I didn't remind them of that. I know they care about me and are worried for me—not to mention their own troubles.

Nan got tired of my evading her direct questions in e-mail and called me in person this morning, right after Grace's call. She's scared to death for me and wants me to come stay with her for a while, or at least think of visiting somewhere out of state. I appreciate everyone's concern, but I can't deal with it.

Cousin Nathan, at least, doesn't know about the current worries. He sent me a fax this morning with a photo he'd taken of Ida Sebran's bakery—he thought I'd like to see it. Very plain, a stucco facade with an ordinary awning out front and CARL'S BAKERY on a sign over the door. He scrawled a note on the fax saying he'd tried to go in and talk to her again, but that she had customers and asked him not to bother her anymore. So it seems that avenue is closed. To him, at least.

I can't believe I'm getting another call. I'm ready to screen it and run over to Jack's Car Rental with apologies for being late, when I hear Aunt Becky's voice from New York. Something's wrong. I grab the phone before she hangs up.

"Ruby, I just wanted to let you know that Uncle Aaron lost his balance and fell down the two steps to the living room. His knee is all twisted and he may have to have an operation."

"I'm here, Aunt Becky," I tell her while I stop the answering machine from beeping.

"Of course you are, dear."

Oh. She thought I was here all the time—I remember that, like Aaron, she doesn't understand machines, either.

"I wasn't going to call the out-of-town relatives, but Nathan said just now that I should call you—that you might want to come up here. I don't think it's necessary, honey. We're hoping for the best, but of course, he's eighty. Like me. We're getting up there. I guess we can expect anything."

"Please give him a hug for me, Aunt Becky. I'm so sorry he's in pain. You were very sweet to call me, and I know how busy you must be going to the hospital. I'll keep posted through Nathan—how's that?"

"He's here. Would you like to talk to him? I have to leave."

She puts Nathan on the phone. He sounds upset.

"I just sent you a fax from the store, Ruby, when Grandma Becky called."

"Can you talk now?"

"Yes, she's gone to take a shower, and then I'll drive

her to the hospital again. I guess it happened early this morning."

"So what's the story?"

"I haven't talked to the doctor, of course, but it doesn't sound like life or death."

"Thank God for that. Still, it's an awful shock. I hate thinking of him in all that pain. I hadn't wanted to tell you this, but I've had some life-and-death issues come up down here. There was an attempt on my life last week, and the police think it's connected somehow to Marla Solomon's murder. At least some of the police do, and I certainly do."

"My God, Ruby, that's awful. Why don't you get out of town?"

"You're the third person to tell me that in one morning. I can't just run away."

"You know that we've been pussyfooting around Uncle Aaron—trying to talk to Ida and Anna and everyone but him. Maybe now he'd be willing to talk to you. Why don't you make a trip to New York? He's not going to talk to me."

"I definitely don't want you telling Aaron or Becky what happened to me, Nathan."

"No, of course I won't."

"Look, if I lived closer, I'd take your advice. But I can't just keep running up there."

"Not under ordinary circumstances, you couldn't. But wake up, Ruby. Give yourself a little breathing room. And besides, it's a perfect excuse. So from Becky's point of view, you'll be a little more of the doting niece than she'd expect you to be—but when she sees you, it'll be a done deal, and she's got other things on her mind. I'm thinking of people in Eternal. If you're visiting a sick relative, it's a legitimate excuse to get out of town. And it might be your only chance."

"I'll think about it. I want you to call me tonight and let me know what the doctor says. I'm feeling awful for Uncle Aaron."

We hang up and I head for the car, at last. Two trips to New York—this is nuts. Not to mention the expense, although I do have enough frequent flyer miles for one more ticket.

I take care of the glitch in Jack's computer system, and agree with him that his car-rental shop might profit from a well-run Web site. It's just a bigger deal than he thinks. I have a couple of friends who can handle it for him—not to mention scores of other techies who'd be glad for the business. The more I ruminate on the idea, the more I think it's probably essential for Jack to compete with the national companies who're already taking on-line reservations. He ought to take the plunge—just not with me right now.

I'm exhausted as I get back in the car and realize that half the day is still ahead. Part of me has definitely not recovered from the run off the mountain road, and I'm dreading the plane trip back and forth to New York. The planes these days are more like Greyhound buses, except that bus seats have lots more room and their windows are twice as large. But I feel a pull toward New York and Uncle Aaron, and I never ignore my hunches.

My favorite police lieutenant calls on the car phone and I try out my new plans on him.

"Go," Paul says in no uncertain terms.

"Why am I not surprised? Everyone seems to think

my problems will just disappear if I leave the city."

"I do want to ask a favor before you go, Ruby. See if the victim's sister will talk to you about the case."

"Essie Sue Margolis? I thought you were going to interview her yourself."

"We did. She made some effort to appear cooperative, but my cop's intuition was buzzing me the whole time. She seemed evasive to me—nervous, and not wanting to talk about Glenda Solomon's past, beyond her college days when she dated Milt."

"She was nervous with me, too, when I asked her to speak with you. But I think it's just residue from the whole trauma of Marla's death. Especially since she's the type to cover up any sign of weakness. I'd be shaky, too, in her shoes, and certainly in a police interview."

"Yeah, I hear you. But do it, okay? Before you leave for New York?"

"Your wish is my command. I have to talk to her anyway, about the trip. So far, I haven't done a thing about the rabbi's installation I'm supposed to help with. She's not going to be thrilled to hear I'm off again."

In very uncharacteristic fashion, I decide to drop in on Essie Sue and Hal on the spur of the moment. I want to get this over with. There's another reason, too. I need to climb back on the horse that threw me, so to speak, and travel that mountain road again. In daylight this time. They do, after all, live in town, and the trip is one I've made many times, unfortunately. In the light of day, it's not a long trek at all.

I feel goose bumps as I very slowly begin the downhill run past that same wooded spot. I survive the ordeal by looking at the road ahead of me and avoiding the scenery on either side. I'm proud of myself.

Essie Sue is very surprised to see me. Ha—that's an understatement, since, needless to say, I never, never drop in. I don't have to worry about catching her in the same stage of undress as she found me the other day. Of course, she wouldn't be caught dead in a Wonder Woman nightshirt, but aside from that, she always prepares for any eventuality by dressing for the day even when she's at home. She's wearing a powder blue matching shirt and pants set.

"Hi," I say, a little sheepishly. Too bad I can't bring off my entrance the way she did when she breezed me out of bed the other day, but I've never been able to compete with Essie Sue in the chutzpah department.

She has no choice but to let me in. I'm so relieved to be getting this over with that I don't even mind interrupting their lunch.

Lunch is what I imagined her noncompany lunch would be—Breakstone's low-fat cottage cheese and a banana for potassium. Hal's plate is the same, with an onion bagel added. It must be Tuesday. I remember he has poppyseed on Monday. I dutifully accept the banana and cottage cheese she offers me without choice. "Women eat the smaller portion, don't we, dear?"

I briefly think of the svelte size I'd be if I lived under her manicured wing—just a wisp of a thing. Wouldn't that be great? No, I guess not. I'd be dead or in jail by now if I lived with the Calorie Dominatrix. No wonder Hal hits the bourbon.

I tell Essie Sue I won't be planning with the rabbi this week, since I'm off to visit a sick relative. I'm mentally putting up my arms in front of my face in self-defense, when I realize she's not horrified. A sudden pang of empathy, maybe? I'm feeling guilty for not giving her credit when I realize she's merely distracted.

"You should go," she says. "Stay awhile."

"Huh?"

Well, maybe not exactly distracted. Maybe something else.

"The police seem to be handling all this quite well," she says. "Have they given you a badge when I wasn't looking?"

"Essie Sue, what's the matter with you?" Hal looks shocked. I'm taken aback, too.

"You got me into another police interview," she says.

"No, I didn't. He asked to see you himself. It wasn't my idea at all."

"I don't like having to talk about my sister's life. It's too painful."

Okay, I better backtrack. She is the victim here, and I know something about pain. But there goes any opportunity of doing what Paul has asked me to do.

"I'm sure it's painful, Essie Sue," I say. "It's just that the police often have to go into tender territory in a murder case. Don't take it personally. Were they insensitive?"

"They were all right."

"She doesn't want to go into the past," Hal pipes up.

"Leave it to me, Hal," she says. If looks could kill, the man would be prone by now. She starts clearing the table, and I recognize my cue to leave. Maybe I'm losing my touch, or maybe I'm just wiped out from recent events, but she wins this round. I'm gone.

chapter
27

....

Uncle Aaron is across the park at Mt. Sinai Hospital, not that far from Aaron and Becky's apartment. I have a tiny overnight bag slung over my shoulder, since I plan to hang around New York no more than a day or two. I'm hoping Becky will invite me to stay, but if things are too hectic, I can crash at Nathan's. My big decision for now is whether I should let the taxi driver drop me at the apartment on Riverside or the hospital on Fifth. I decide the hospital.

It's amazing—I just arrived, and I'm already wistful about having to leave. I love poking around in the old bookstores downtown, and at this time in particular, I could sure use the comfort of being by myself in my favorite haunts. Some people yearn for soul food when they've just gone through a crisis—I need food for my soul. An hour surrounded by old volumes would make me feel more like my real self than any healing process the best doctor could prescribe for me. This is the most *me* there is.

Things ring true for me in this city. Despite the reputation of the place, there's really less bull being shot. I often remind myself of that when I'm away from New York and imprisoned in the midst of some discussion about self-actualization or how to relieve boredom. Who has time to be bored? My problem is how to squeeze in another book or how to have time to think very hard about something I want to think about. As for self-actualization, what's to actualize? You can't make something from nothing, and a self sure ain't gonna appear just because you've decided to actualize it.

We pull up to the front portico of the hospital by five o'clock, and I head for the admissions desk to talk my way into visiting during nonvisiting hours. It doesn't work, but I meet a soul mate who's waiting in line, and she simply tells me the obvious. "Look as though you belong here. Who has time to check?" Enough said.

Uncle Aaron looks old and frail in the bed. There's lots of white space on either side of him, and I have to admit to myself that he doesn't take up as much space as he did in his own dining room. His face brightens when he sees me, and it's suddenly worth everything just to be here.

"No," I say to him. "You're not dying just because I've crossed the country to see you—I promise you that."

He laughs. "I was so pleased to see you I wasn't thinking," he says, "but I'm sure I would have wondered soon enough. Whatever the reason, you look so good to me."

"Aunt Becky doesn't know I was coming. Will she be here later?"

"Sometimes Nathan brings her back after he closes the shop, and sometimes she's too tired to come twice."

"I'll have to call and ask her if I can stay at the apartment. I'll only be here for a day or two."

"Don't worry about it. She'll love to have you. And you know she always keeps those spare rooms spruced up enough for the Queen of England, so there's nothing she has to do to get ready."

I find out the knee's in better shape than first expected, and surgery might not be required, thank goodness. He doesn't seem overly medicated, and apparently, he's just had a nap. There's no question this is the time to do my talking. If I call Becky too soon, she might come down here or send someone for me, so I decide just to sit down beside him, go for it and call her later. The problem is I really don't want to burden him with too much information to worry about. I'll have to do some creative talking.

"Uncle Aaron, you remember on my last trip I was asking about the old days in the union, when you were friendly with Irv and Carl Sebran? There were things you didn't want to talk to me about because of confidences you'd been asked to keep. Would you consider changing your mind if I told you it was very, very important to me?"

"Is this why you came?"

"I wanted to see how you were, but yes, I also felt a sense of urgency about what happened to the Sebran brothers. I know it's a lot to ask. I can't tell you everything, but I can tell you that my interest involves the accident that killed Stu. I've recently found out that he was warned just before his death to stay away from Milt Aboud's bakery. The only connection Stu and Milt had from the past was their two families' friendship from the union days. I need to know what happened between the brothers. I've tried to spare you by asking Irv's ex-wife Anna, and she told me quite a bit, but Irv never told her what actually made Carl drop his lawsuit and move to New Jersey. Carl's wife Ida probably knows, but I'm not close enough to find out. You're my only hope at this point."

I've decided to stake everything on the Stu connection, not only because Aaron is Stu's blood relative but also because since Stu's already dead, his safety won't be a worrying point. What's happened to me and to Milt will not only complicate matters but will certainly upset Aaron and Becky to a much greater degree. I just don't feel it's necessary. What I've told him so far doesn't make a lot of sense, mainly because I don't have the answers myself. Rationally, he ought to question me a lot more. Hell, I would in his shoes. But I'm betting he won't.

Aaron's a smart cookie, but one thing I've learned about the aged is that some of them develop the art of going beyond smart. What I've made is an emotional appeal, not a rational one, and it'll come down to a matter of trust.

He thinks about it for a long time with his eyes closed. So long that I'm hoping he hasn't dozed off. He hasn't.

"You're telling me you need this information badly?"

"So badly I'm asking you to betray a confidence you made to two men who are dead now."

I'm putting it on the line here—I owe him that much. Aaron had the strength of character to keep this secret for many years. Any pretense on my part would be disrespectful of who he is and what he might be betraying.

He gestures for me to help shift his covers. I give him a glass of water with a straw. He sips and looks up at me at the same time, like Joshie drinking Kool-Aid at seven. I almost expect him to blow bubbles.

"They're both dead now, but that doesn't give me an excuse," he says, all grown up.

"I know."

"I tried not to be in the middle of their feud, but this is what Irv told me. Carl later confirmed it. When Carl's lawyer sent papers ordering Irv to close his bakery until the lawsuit between them was settled, Irv saw his new business and his means of support going down the drain. He was desperate. He went that very morning down to the union offices and talked behind closed doors with the president.

"Maybe Nathan or I already told you this when you asked about the old days, but in all of the New York City area, there were only three hundred members of the Bagel Bakers Union. No one was allowed to divulge recipes to non-union members, and with so few bakeries to feed a city hungry for the bagels they'd known in Europe, all the union members did well. Membership was not only passed down from father to son, but only the sons of members were permitted to join the union at all.

"Max Sebran, Irv and Carl's father, had registered

them for membership as soon as they finished school and began working full-time in the bakery. He told them, as we were all told by our fathers, that this was a fortunate birthright. Only it proved not so lucky for Carl."

Uncle Aaron tried to lie farther down in the bed, but anything more than a slump was obviously causing him pain.

"Do you want me to have the nurse help you? We can take a break," I tell him, "or you can put it off." I'm feeling guilty now.

"No, I'm okay. I seem to be glad to get it off my chest, Ruby. That's a surprise to me."

I don't know what to say to that, so I keep going.

"You said it wasn't so lucky for Carl." Getting us back on track. I hate myself when I'm like this, but we're getting so close.

"Irv told the union president behind closed doors that Carl was not Max Sebran's son."

Uncle Aaron had his eyes closed now, as if his words were visible, like comic book words, and he didn't want to see them.

"Irv was born right here in New York City. Carl, though, had come over from Europe with Max and his wife Clara when he was two years old. He was a cousin. His mother had died in childbirth, and the father had begged Max to give the toddler a chance in America. Max and Clara were a young couple with no children yet, and they brought the boy on the ship with them from Europe. They raised both boys as their own, as brothers.

"Max never told the boys the truth until he was on his deathbed, years after Clara had died. He told them he had raised them as brothers, and brothers they should remain. He had written a will leaving everything to them, share and share alike.

"You have to remember, Ruby, that in those days this was a very common thing. Mixed families came over from the old country all the time. I'm surprised Max and Clara didn't tell them earlier as a matter of course, but they didn't. Maybe they didn't want to encourage adolescent competition or jealousy. By the time they *were* told, they were already members of the union, and the subject never came up."

"What subject?" I'm so engrossed, I'm not being all that sharp. Then it hits me.

"Oy," is all I can manage.

"Oy is right. Only one boy had the birthright."

Uncle Aaron is trying to sit up now. "Irv told me later it had never been discussed, not with Max or between Irv and Carl after Max died. I'm not sure if Carl ever even thought about it."

"But Irv did."

"Irv certainly did. He said he never gave it a second thought in the year after Max died, when the boys shared Max's bakery. Or even after he moved out on his own. But when Carl first started haranguing him about appropriating Max's secret recipes, Irv said it popped into his mind one day as an amazing act of chutzpah. Here was his brother trying to keep him from using their father's recipes, when Max wasn't even Carl's real father. Carl couldn't even be in the union if they knew."

"Did he talk to Carl about that?"

"No. He said that they both took their cue from Max, and it didn't feel right to mention what Max had made unmentionable."

I ask Aaron again if he's too tired. He says no, so I try to hurry things along myself. I know I shouldn't keep him too long. I'm encouraged, though, by his demeanor. Telling me seems to be doing him good.

"Irv told me he kept the union thing to himself all during the time he was getting those papers from Carl's lawyer. It just made him madder, but it never occurred to him to use the secret against Carl. He always thought he'd win any lawsuit—that Carl was being sold a bill of goods by a bad lawyer. But the day he was served papers to close his bakery—this was a whole new level. He knew his customers could go elsewhere, and that he'd never be able to keep up the rent and the expenses if the store wasn't bringing in any money.

"Irv told me he woke up the next morning and knew what he had to do without batting an eyelash."

"Well, surely the union would have had a lot to consider. This sort of thing doesn't happen every day, and Max had kept the whole thing a secret from his boys all those years. It wasn't Carl's fault in any way, even if he did sue his brother over business."

"You're thinking from a nineties point of view, Rubelah. This was the nineteen forties. Businessmen didn't consider feelings so much. They don't now, either, for that matter—they just have more language that covers up what they're doing. Like when they terminate someone and send an Exit Counselor to mop up."

"Fair enough. But what did the union do when they found out?"

"Well, the president went to his board, and they were furious."

"With Carl? With Irv for finking?"

"With Max. A lot of the families had brought cousins over from Europe—cousins who could have made a good living in the business. But everyone knew the rule. Only sons were in. Limiting the competition was the whole point. Max knew that as well as anyone else. He cheated."

"Did Max adopt Carl?"

"What adoption? Carl was never formally adopted, and it wouldn't have made any difference. Carl was out. The guys got together and Carl was out. Like that.

"One of the officers went over to see Carl and told him that very afternoon. Irv never saw him again. I don't know that he tried."

"Did Carl talk to you?"

"He did. He said some bitter things. I don't need to go into it. You know all you need to know about it, don't you?"

"Yes, and I'm grateful. Maybe I can explain to you how I think this will help me get to the bottom of Stu's accident."

Aaron slides back down under the covers.

"Could I have a little more water?" he asks me.

He only takes a sip. "Ruby, honey, I trust you to do whatever you have to do with the information. But I have ups and downs about it. Right now I'm down, and I'm tired."

"I'm sorry, Uncle Aaron. It's the hardest thing I ever had to ask you. I'm kind of tired, too, from the flight. Could I sit here and hold your hand for a while? And we won't talk?"

"I'd like that. You can call Becky in a little while. Sit

here and put your legs up. It's a big bed."

I go around to the other side of the bed, with plenty of white space, slip off my shoes, and stretch out beside him.

chapter
28
....

I'm pleased—Nathan is actually taking off work and driving me to Jersey. I'm flying out of Newark in a few hours, and he's agreed to take a detour and run me by Ida Sebran's bakery in Jersey City before we head for the airport. My suggestion, not his. In fact, he's not keen on it. Since the idea only popped into my mind just now when I realized we had some time to kill, I'm tickled that I was able to talk him into it.

"She was shut up tighter than a drum last time I saw her, Ruby. I can't imagine that she'll have anything to say to you."

"She likes Aaron and Becky," I say, trying to make my plan sound more rational than it really is. "And none of us are related to Irv's family, so we don't pose a threat to her peace of mind. I'm certainly not going to mention Milt or his mother. So who knows? People open up to me sometimes."

"I'm not surprised. But don't count your chickens, okay?"

We make our way quickly out of the city—heading for the Lincoln Tunnel.

"You're so sweet to your grandparents," I say. "I don't know what they'd do without you. Becky told me last night you're helping her clean out the last of the walk-in closets in the apartment."

"Yeah, she thinks that Aaron's being in the hospital is a signal sent by the Almighty that she needs to get everything in order. These two have been so extraordinarily healthy that I told them they're spoiled. It doesn't mean the end has come just because he's wrenched his knee."

"Still, they're not youngsters."

"I know. But my hunch is they've got a few years yet. Aaron's doing fine—he really is. And Becky's making me the custodian of the family photographs, so she knew I wouldn't mind helping with the closet."

I get that tinge of sadness that always comes over me when I realize how young Stu was when he died. Here are Becky and Aaron in their eighties together. I guess Nathan's reading my mind. He reaches over the front seat and takes my hand.

We're out of the tunnel, by Hoboken, and I take one more wistful look back across the Hudson to see the Manhattan skyline.

"Thanks for humoring me today," I say. "I know it's hard for you to take time off during the day."

"It was selfish," he says. "I wouldn't have missed hearing the story of Carl's ouster from the union for anything. I could hardly wait until this morning so you could tell me."

Nathan looks a lot like his grandfather. He has Aaron's impish smile. I'm trying to fill him in on everything as fast as possible, and I'm feeling bad that we live half a country apart.

"It must have been really tricky for Aaron and Becky to remain friends with both brothers and their wives after all this happened," I say. "Becky told me they used to invite Carl and Ida and their family over once in a while, and that they'd always ask who was coming before they accepted."

"I just thought of something," Nathan says. "How was Irv able to pass down the business to his three daughters and their husbands?"

"By the time the daughters were grown, the union was long gone," I say.

"You've become quite an expert," Nathan teases.

"You might say I'm obsessed," I answer. "Almost getting killed twice will do that to you." As soon as I say it, I'm sorry. I've spent two days trying to allay Nathan's fears, and now I'm frightening him again. I must be really tired. "Forget that for now," I tell him. "Please."

"What can I say? I've said it all, but you insist on going back so soon."

"I have to." I change the subject. "I thought you and Becky were going to fall out last night when you walked into the hospital room and saw us dozing."

"We were bowled over. I got a kick out of Becky saying that was the last place she expected to find a beautiful woman sleeping with her husband."

"That even got a smile out of Uncle Aaron."

We pull up in front of Carl's Bakery, the familiar building with the awning, looking just like the photo Nathan had sent me. An old woman is outside, wiping the glass door to the entrance. I remember Nathan's description, and he doesn't have to tell me it's Ida Sebran.

"Ida, it's Nathan Rothman. I came over last month."

She puts wet hands on her hips and stares at us. Her bra strap's showing, and I think at once of Milt's mother Anna's description of the safety pin. I don't dare mention the Abouds, of course. She might even want to hear about Anna for all I know, but I can't chance it.

"Do you remember Stu Rothman, Mrs. Sebran? Aaron and Becky's nephew? I'm his widow, and I'm gathering a family history." I don't know *where* that came from. I'm suddenly really, really sorry I made Nathan bring me here, but that doesn't stop me from trying to salvage something.

"I know all of you were friends, and I just thought since I was visiting, I'd take back some goodies from your bakery, and get to meet you."

I'm an idiot. She looks at me as if I'm crazy.

"Whose widow?" she asks Nathan, ignoring me.

"My uncle, Stu Rothman. He would have been the same age as your children, I imagine."

"My children don't live here anymore. My daughter and son have moved away. I told you not to come back."

I begin the mopping-up procedure. "Just thought we'd stop by. Can I buy some of those muffins I see in the window?"

"You're not looking for a friends' discount, are you? I don't give discounts. Not to family—not to friends."

"Oh no. I want to pay full price."

She seems mollified. I leave Nathan in the car and run in with her. I come out loaded with several dozen of anything I can grab, and say good-bye.

"Throw it in the backseat," Nathan says as we pull away. We look at each other and laugh, finally. We're so relieved to be out of there, we're both giddy.

"Want anything to eat?" I say.

"Are you kidding? I'll stick to my bagels. *Oy*, that's not even funny, considering what happened to her, is it?" he says. "But no thank you. I had a sample last time I was here. It wasn't cheap, either. I'll bet she charged you retail plus."

"Guilt money," I say. "Who's counting? I would have paid her anything she asked, believe me. You were right and I was stupid. I'm sorry."

"Well, at least you got to see her in person. It's as close as you'll get to that family, since Carl's dead and I'm certainly not taking you there again."

"I'm glad I saw her, now that I'm so involved in all this. Carl and Irv's generation will be gone soon—all of them. I was able to spend time with Irv's wife Anna, and in some weird way, I wanted to meet Carl's wife, too. Now I have, even if it didn't yield anything."

We zoom out to the airport with no problems, since it's not even two o'clock and the traffic's in a lull—a lull on these freeways means not quite bumper-to-bumper. I kiss Nathan good-bye at the departure entrance.

"I wish I could do something more for you," he says as I shoulder my travel bag and prepare to make a run for it.

"You've done more than I'd ever have a right to expect," I tell him.

"But it hasn't added up to anything. I wanted to do something that would make a difference."

Neither of us knows just how prophetic that statement will be.

chapter
29

....

I must be home because I'm sitting under a tin roof in a huge picnic shelter, trapped in a hailstorm with twenty-one five-year-olds and three frazzled religious schoolteachers while Rabbi Kapstein screams the story of Noah's Ark. His voice is several decibels louder than the Ping-Pong-sized hailstones on the tin roof, but no one's listening. Which is a good thing because he's just reached a crescendo in which the world is washed away by water, thunder, and lightning. Call me crazy, but isn't the subject matter just a tad alarming, under the circumstances? I think I'm hallucinating, but no such luck.

Half the kids are running around on a sugar high from the jelly doughnuts, gumdrops, and Hi-C. The rest of them are crying—they're scared of the storm. Kevin would know that if he hadn't insisted on preaching from the bandstand several feet above them and five feet back.

I'm flashing back to a Succoth tent at a camp-out long ago, when I walked in on Stu curled up in a circle of

little kids, his arms around the ones next to him—the others leaning on his legs. He was telling the story of the Feast of Booths, shelters in the desert night.

It's not only the body language that defines the two men, it's the bodies themselves. Stu was flexible, easy around kids. Kevin's rigid, tight—his body demanding that ever-present respect. At most, he'll put a child on his lap and shake his knee up and down beaming not at the child, but at the parent who's the beneficiary of the gesture. He thinks the children love it when he throws his voice into pyrotechnics. I've noticed the blazing fall-out dazzles him, not the kids. The kids, I think, would just like to know him.

In Central Texas, it's flood or drought—take your choice. Either the water table is at rock bottom, or brimming over. Sometimes both in the same year. This year the ground has been dry and hard for the last three months, and now the rain is falling so fast it can only run off into all the wrong places. When I left my house this afternoon, the day was hot and sunny—now it's hot and torrential.

I came home from New York to find three messages from Kevin on my answering machine—apparently Essie Sue hadn't told him about my trip. Ha—could she be slipping? Not likely. Since time is closing in on us, Kevin asked me to meet him at the picnic, where we'd have plenty of time to huddle on the sidelines and make plans. Not. Little did I know I'd become one of the teachers as soon as I hit the premises. They brought only three teachers for this crowd? Give me a break. My personal ratio with preschool children is five to one with

five-year-olds, four to one with four-year-olds, and so on down. Babies one to one, definitely.

I'm sitting on the floor with four of the crying ones. This is one less than my ratio—I should be taking care of five, and I'm wondering which poor teacher has six. I have to confess to my kids that it's a little scary for me, too. There are no sides to this shelter, and the rain is coming in horizontally. We're all huddled in the center of the space trying to keep dry.

Kevin has now come to the part about the animals two by two, which is a heck of a lot less threatening than death by water, and I wish they could hear him. But by now the noise inside and the clatter on the roof is drowning him out completely. If he were down here with the rest of us, he could take four or five kids himself, but it's no use expecting miracles. He's talking rainbows by now, I'm sure.

We have an hour before it's time for the picnic to end. I decide to go for favorite music—songs always cheer me up. The kids tell their favorite Jewish songs—five-year-old fashion—"I Have a Little Dreidel" and such, and we all sing them in turn. By my clock, that takes a total of about sixty seconds.

Okay, this is an emergency. The heck with the Jewish content. We're telling jokes. I forgot how much five-year-olds love jokes.

It works.

I get a few minutes with Kevin after all the mother have finally made it through the rain to pick up their kids. I'm not in the best of moods.

"Kevin, what is it specifically that you need my help

on? Do you want to go over your speech, or the order of the ceremony, or what?"

"I wanted you to know what I've done so far."

Hey, this is great. I didn't think I'd get off this easy. I'm excellent at listening.

"First we're having a processional, with all the members of the board marching up to the pulpit after me."

I gulp. "Okay." Odd, but I can take it.

"In black robes." His eyes glaze over. He's picturing it, I guess. "With the choir singing as we go down."

He must be thinking coronation, not installation. Our choir consists of Mr. Goldberg, Mrs. Farber, and Mr. Chernoff. They have their hands full singing "Adon Olam." I don't think they're up for this.

"Followed by visiting dignitaries."

"Uh-huh." I don't want to know who the dignitaries are.

"Suitable music, suitable prayer book selections, then my installation address. What do you think so far?"

"Stu just had everyone come to a Friday night service."

"Your husband and I, from what I can ascertain, were very different." You can say that again. I'm remembering all the people who were drawn to Stu because they knew he was truly interested in their lives.

"Unlike your husband, I believe we were chosen not in small part because of our style. We bring a sense of dignity to the congregation. Of formality. Of respect that has been sorely missed."

His "style," so far as I can tell, consists of charging straight into people. And what's this "our" style? "Beg

pardon, but is this the imperial 'we' you're talking about, Kevin?"

"Please, can you manage to call me 'rabbi' when we're discussing a congregational event?"

"Get a grip, Kevin. I think you ought to tone down the ceremonies here."

"I'm not asking for your input."

"So why did you call me a zillion times and drag me to the Kindergarten Picnic from Hell?"

"To carry out my plans."

"Kevin, I'm wet, I'm hungry, and I'm insulted. The only thing I'm carrying out tonight is an anchovy pizza."

chapter 30

....

Reality breaks in on me early—the phone rings from New York at six-thirty in the morning. I don't think at *all* at six-thirty in the morning, but on the other hand, it's just as well. The juxtaposition of last week's planning for visiting dignitaries while my life was the bull's-eye for someone's target practice left me with double vision. I need to focus on what's vital.

"Ruby, it's Aunt Becky."

I immediately get a glitch in my stomach.

"Is Uncle Aaron all right?"

"Yes, darling. I didn't mean to frighten you. He's home and lumbering all over the place. In other words, we're back to normal."

"I know you're not always up this early, so I was worried," I say.

"I set my alarm to call at seven-thirty because I get better long-distance rates that way before eight o'clock. I figured seven-thirty wouldn't be too early for you."

"Right." How could I forget that New Yorkers who aren't business people just naturally assume the whole country is on their time? It's no use telling Aunt Becky we're an hour earlier here—she'd never remember.

"Uncle Aaron thought I should call you. Why, I don't know. I think he might be slipping, Ruby. I told him to call you himself, but you know how he hates the telephone. I knew he wouldn't."

"What's up?"

"Just to tell you I had a telephone call yesterday from Ida Sebran—Carl Sebran's widow. From New Jersey."

My stomach's doing it again.

"We talk every once in a while on the phone, Ruby. They were peculiar people, and after the brothers broke up, Ida and Carl and their children would never come to our house for one of our big get-togethers because they knew Irv and his family might be there. We always invited everybody. So we used to invite Carl's family over separately. Just now and then. Our children were close in age."

"So what did Ida say?" I know Becky has to be kept on track—her digressions are famous.

"She said you'd been to her shop, Ruby. I told her it was news to me."

Uh-oh. I guess Nathan didn't say anything to them. I certainly don't want her to think I went behind her back. Actually, I wasn't thinking of her one way or another.

"I'm sorry I didn't mention it, Aunt Becky, but I couldn't have, because I just decided to do it on the spur of the moment when Nathan was driving me to Newark airport. I got a better deal ticketing out of Newark this time, so that's where I flew in and out."

"So why did you go to Ida's?"

"It's hard to say. Partly because we had some time to kill, and I knew we were near Jersey City. You know how fascinated I've been hearing the stories of the old union days, and since I had the chance to visit Milt's mother, I thought I'd like to meet Carl's wife, too."

Pretty lame, but the truth is I didn't have a very clear reason for going, except for curiosity. And a hunch that it might be important in some way. One thing's for sure—I certainly overestimated my ability to make friends with Ida.

"Well, she's a peculiar woman, Ruby. I told you that. She seemed upset that you visited her. Aaron says she's kind of paranoid. He seems upset that you visited her, too."

"Did she say why she was upset?"

I'm really sorry I've worried Uncle Aaron, but since he's not on the phone, I can't think of anything else I can do about it at the moment.

"Ida said she didn't like people poking into her business, and that Nathan had already paid one visit to her. I talked to him about it and he said he'd been in the area one day, and just wanted to keep up some links to their family."

The two of us are a great pair for lame excuses. And I'll get blamed being older and putting Nathan up to it. As rightly I should.

"Anything else?"

"She said you were trying to find out about her children, and they won't like that—one of the reasons they both moved away was to get away from people prying."

"She *must* be paranoid, Aunt Becky. I don't know

anything *about* her children. Nathan said her children and Stu were about the same age. Then she said they had moved away, and that was it."

"It's getting close to eight o'clock now, and I mostly called because Aaron wanted me to. I'm trying to humor him since he's been home from the hospital. And of course, I'm always glad to talk to you."

"I don't want to keep you, Aunt Becky. I'm so glad Uncle Aaron's better, and please, please tell him not to worry about anything. Everything is fine here. I'm really sorry if I disturbed your old friend Ida."

"Oh, don't worry about Ida. She's crazy."

I have to laugh after we hang up. She had me plotzing when she first called—thinking I'd really blown it with both of them. Now she seems to be putting it out of her mind. Maybe that's how she's lived as long as she has.

I'm sure Ida is a bit crazy, but I'm taking no chances. I dial Nathan long distance at the bakery.

"I was just getting ready to call you," he says, "but I thought you might be asleep."

"Don't I wish. Becky just called, and told me Ida was really upset."

"Yeah, I know all about it. I hadn't told them about either visit I'd made."

"I'm sorry I got you into any of this, but honestly, I had nowhere else to go, and I still can't be *too* sorry, if you know what I mean."

"I know what you mean. Don't worry about it."

"Becky said one thing that I don't get, Nathan. She said Ida was concerned about my interest in her children. I don't remember *being* interested in her children."

"Maybe she just drew conclusions when you said you were compiling a family history."

"*Oy*, I forgot I even said that. I was just trying to think of an excuse to be there. I should have listened to you. It was a really bad idea."

"No harm done. I'm going to see Aaron and Becky tomorrow night to help clean out the walk-in closet, and I'll try to smooth things over for both of us."

"You're a doll. And if you get the chance while you're cleaning out mementos, keep the conversation going about the old days, okay? Now I'm interested in why Ida was so disturbed, other than her general craziness."

"So you want me to get myself *back* into hot water, huh, Ruby?"

"In a way, I do. I want to know more. No—don't do it. The last thing I want to do is put a strain on the easy relationship you have with your grandparents."

"Strain, schmain. You know damn well neither one of us is going to stop. Are you sure you're not my blood relative? Maybe the yenta gene comes down through marriage. Check you later, alligator."

"Am I lucky to have you. Call me if anything comes up."

"I'll do better than that. I'll fax you any interesting photos I find at my grandparents' house—like the one of Ida's shop I faxed you."

"Becky's giving you the lot?"

"Anything I want for my photo collection."

"Your little Museum of Bagels? Hey, maybe it'll be famous some day."

E-mail from: Ruby
To: Nan
Subject: *Weekend of Woe*

Almost time for the LSAT, right? I'm rooting for you, babe. I really admire you for taking on the prep for that along with your regular work. Can't wait to hear about it—I'm betting you ace it.

I'm glad I've been filling you in night by night—and it's sure a lot cheaper than long distance. In answer to your last question—everything's in place here. I don't hang out at the bakery since Milt and I are supposedly at odds over our partnership finances. Lieutenant Lundy continues to think it's prudent to give the impression I'm keeping my nose out of Milt's life, whether it's his family or his business. I'm trying to take care of myself, and that's all I can do.

Talking to Nathan today cheered me up, and I needed it—I have a harrowing weekend ahead. Tomorrow I'm spending the day with Turner Goldman, who's back in town from his trial in Oklahoma. Turner, Milt, and I are meeting off the record at Turner's law offices. I'm no lawyer, but Turner wants me there. He feels I have Milt's confidence and that I can help. Turner's also convinced that the police case against Milt is stalled because of all the new twists and turns, and that they really don't have enough evidence against him to go forward. I'll believe it when I see it.

And Sunday night—well, Sunday night is payback time, NanO. I agreed to Essie Sue's deal that if she'd have another voluntary interview with the police, I'd *let* myself be escorted by Rabbi Kapstein to the fund-raising ball. She had the interview, and it yielded nothing. Expect the same from my end of the deal.

chapter
31

....

"Quiet, ladies and gentlemen. Shhh."

Essie Sue's voice whispers from the loudspeaker.
Even though the congregation is still buzzing noisily below her, she's on her best behavior. Maybe she's over-
awed by the full house in the social hall for tonight's
installation ceremony. Just as I'm about to award her
kudos for decorum, she scrapes her talons on the microphone in a gesture calculated to simulate either crashing
freight trains or the screeching of chalk pieces on a thousand blackboards. It gets their attention.

"That's better. Thank you all for cooperating with
your silence."

Cooperating? We're all catatonic from the microphone blast. Essie Sue is wearing a long, white sequined
gown for the ball, which follows this event, and she's
standing up there alone, which can only mean one thing.
Kevin got his way and we're having a processional. I

blame myself for being too preoccupied to fight this—not that I had much chance of winning.

She raises her arm, points a long red fingernail toward the back rows, and the doors open. Kevin, in white-robed splendor, leads off with one of those old-time bridal paces—step, stop, step, stop. Say it isn't so. He's followed by the choir—augmented from three members to four—whose anthem is fortunately drowned out by the crowd, which is definitely not cooperating.

Be glad for small favors—at least they decided the sanctuary was too small for the installation. I find peace in there, and now it won't be ruint, as the bubbas would say.

The processional is ecumenical—I count all the requisite faiths. Our temple board of directors follows, black-robed. They look less than thrilled—Essie Sue must have used force. Buster Copeland's ostrich-skin dress boots flash rebelliously from beneath his robe. All march to the reserved front rows, where Essie Sue joins them. Kevin kisses her and ascends the podium with four of the guest speakers. I'm not sure I'm seeing this right, but he seems to be wearing white faille slippers, like spats, which match the robe and are somehow fastened around his wing tips. Vanity, thy name is Velcro.

Our ecumenical guests are assigned to read psalms and proverbs—many, many psalms and proverbs. The congregation is drifting off. I've seen guests of honor totally done in by too many speeches before the main event, but I've never seen anyone sabotage *himself.* Kevin did plan this, I keep reminding myself.

Finally, he steps to the microphone—or almost steps, before one of the Velcroed slippers comes apart and lies there on the floor. He stares at it. There's a collective gasp—I think people are taking bets on what he'll do about it. At any rate, the spat has split. I'm deciding whether he'll ignore it or slip the other one off, too, when he goes back to his chair, sits down, and sticks his leg out—in two-year-old-boy fashion.

The other speakers are frozen in their seats. He seems to be regally gesturing that the slipper be put back on him. No one moves. He nods imperiously at poor Mrs. Farber, the soprano, who also happens to be the only woman up there. She looks stricken, but kneels—actually kneels—before him and puts on the slipper. She has arthritis so she has to be helped back up by a priest and a minister.

We all settle back in our seats and try to forget—the way one hopes that a brief nightmare won't disturb a whole night's sleep. Kevin gingerly shuffles his way to the microphone. Nan will never believe this.

"My many friends and our special patroness, Mrs. Margolis," he begins. "How can I count the ways in which I may add my own unique contributions to our congregation's illustrious history?" He then counts them. He's listing at least ten years' worth of ways, but as far as I know, he only has a three-year contract, so I decide to put most of them on hold.

He's certainly made good use of his Bartlett's—we're treated to a spate of illustrative quotations, *long* quotations, from Martin Luther King Jr., Benjamin Franklin, Wordsworth, the Dalai Lama, Moses, and many more. Kevin has apparently not heard the old adage, "If you don't strike oil in twenty minutes, stop boring." I fade in and out, mostly out.

I'm faintly aware that he's into the climax of his address—I hear him say, "We must accept the call to action whenever it comes," when a phone rings. A loud phone. It seems to be emanating from Kevin's robe. We're all awake by now. He reaches into the white folds and pulls out—yep, a cell phone. With a beaming smile, he "accepts the call." Aside from Mary Baker Eddy's red phone, which is supposed to ring from her grave on that Final Day, I'm not aware of any other digital deification. Is this the "special surprise" he hinted to me, or is there something worse coming? And I wonder who his confederate was on the other phone—a corporeal one, I hope.

He's winding up now, and if not, he's all wound up at any rate. No one has moved since the phone rang, and he's still grinning over his with-it coup. "We must use the mode of the modern world, ladies and gentlemen. Listen and ye shall hear."

I think I'll stick with the shofar. I can just imagine the look on Stu's face if he'd seen this. The program finally ends with an announcement that the ball will begin soon, and Kevin descends to the reserved rows. The processional becomes the recessional as the rabbi and his board members pass through a shell-shocked audience. I'm thinking no one has noticed that I'm not in the reserved rows as a member of the board. Let's just say I'm not a processional person.

I'm wrong. Kevin has noticed. To my utter horror, he stops at my row and wags his finger at me. I look furiously down at my feet. It doesn't work. The people in my row, formerly friends, are pushing me over their knees toward the aisle where Kevin is waiting. Where the whole recessional is waiting. I suspect my row mates are less interested in Kevin's demands than they are in getting the show on the road, so there's not much I can do to, like—disappear. I'm thinking he just wants to force me into line with the board, but no.

"My date for the ball," he announces with a boom. Essie Sue applauds. Fortunately, everyone else is too stunned to join in. He crooks his elbow like a vise—a gesture as formal as the hesitation step he's doing down the aisle. He's caught my arm in a death grip, and as I'm pulled along to the social hall like the Bride of Frankenstein, I know there must be some Jewish brand of Karma no one told me about.

I'm pretending I'm invisible, and it's not working, so I play a game with myself. I'm calculating how many Valium I might collect from the two hundred beaded evening bags in the room and whether it'll make a lethal dose.

The visible me is, unfortunately, dancing with Kevin *alone*—that's *by ourselves* in front of everybody. We're the First Couple, and are leading off with the First Dance. He calls it dancing. I don't. The spats were fortunately shed with the robe, and he's in formal wear. Tails, to be precise. The only man in the room in tails, but who's counting? Nothing can faze me now—I'm numb. Well, that's not quite true—I'm not too numb to feel acute pain when he stomps on my toes. And also not too numb to be mortified that people I once considered to be sane are actually whispering and speculating that maybe we're An Item.

I'm glad I wore black tonight—it suits my mood. It was also the only thing I had to wear—a long black skirt and a beaded top. My uniform for formals. Kevin, in his new role as my date, is critical of my outfit.

"Red would have gone well with my tux," he says.

"You want red? You'll get red," I say, looking around for something sharp. I end our First Dance before the orchestra does, but it's not that easy to get away from him. I even become extremely sociable, talking intimately to perfect strangers.

Essie Sue can't do enough for me. Sensing I've had it up to here, she stations herself at my right hand and shepherds me from group to group, being solicitous and complimentary and the whole schmear.

"You're marvelous, my dear," she croons in my ear. "The two of you are a wonderful couple. You're making this an unforgettable evening for the rabbi."

"For me, too." Oh, yeah—definitely for me, too. She knows she's got me for tonight, but she's smart enough to know I could blow at any minute.

"You might think this is a payback for the police interview you did as a favor to me, Essie Sue, but you're wrong. Nothing as mundane as an empty interview could pay me back for tonight."

"I know," she says in a moment of honesty, which she obviously instantly regrets. She goes back on the record. "Everyone accepts the fact that I'm a top-notch match-maker. You don't know it now, but you'll be thanking me later." Much later.

"You deserved this wonderful evening, too, Ruby. You've had such a terrible time of it."

"And this is my great reward?"

"You have to admit I've outdone myself. I'm determined to make Marla's memory live."

"Oh, it will."

Out of the corner of my eye I see my date headed out the door. Could it be he's going home? Meeting someone for a tryst on the Levy patio?

No such luck. Essie Sue steps up to the bandstand.

"Ladies and Gentlemen, your attention please. I promised you a surprise. If you'll stop your dancing for a moment and face the front doors, our own Rabbi Kapstein will give you a preview of coming attractions. If you'll give me a moment to assist him, I'll ask the orchestra to provide us with a fanfare."

The doors open and the drums roll. A life-sized beaver-board cutout of a strange-looking creature in royal robes is making its way toward us, rocking from side to side. The rabbi is valiantly attempting to steer the figure from behind, but it's bigger than he is, and he's definitely losing the struggle.

Essie Sue, now right behind him, grabs the figure from his sweating hands and hoists it shoulder-high. I can't believe she's put together this thing.

"It's not *that* heavy," she says, glaring at Kevin.

The figure's face is a cutout sixteen-by-twenty color portrait of the deceased Marla, which, take my word for it, is really creepy. The body is draped in something questionable that must have come straight from the Third Avenue Thrift Shoppe. It smells of mothballs, and it's a gruesome fuschia.

Buster Copeland's voice breaks through the crowd. "I'll be damned," he says. "I thought the thing would be in marble. You have my vote for wherever you want to put this. It ought to save us about six thousand pounds of stone and a hellava lot more in money."

Essie Sue ignores him. "My friends, I want to present a mock-up of the Queen Esther statue which will eventually grace our entrance steps. The borrowed gown is merely to establish a three-dimensional effect for your perusal."

The room is silent. I can only assume that whatever finally appears in the neutral tones of marble will be a lot less scary than the apparition before us.

"Rabbi Kapstein graciously offered to build this motivational substitute for the real thing, until we can afford the initial designs of the sculptor," Essie Sue tells us. "I think we should all give him a hearty round of applause." So Kevin did it—not Essie Sue. Somehow I knew the same brain that could whip out a fund-raising plan worthy of the U.S. Treasury could put together a better Queen Esther than this.

Kevin bows as if the acclaim were actually forthcoming, but we're too appalled to react. Essie Sue, not about to lose the moment, motions Stan Brown and his Band of Renown to strike up the music. Stu and I once tried to tell Stan that the name had been taken, but all he said was, "So sue me." One hundred bar mitzvahs later, no one has.

My date and I are dancing again—if you can call it that—when Turner Goldman cuts in. I could kiss him.

Kevin graciously releases me. "I should go work the room," he tosses out to both of us.

"Did I hear that right?" Turner groans as the song ends. "I think we're all so used to your husband's low-key style, we don't know how to deal with this type. Is this modern?"

"Modern? You mean, is this what they're turning out lately? I doubt it."

I try to keep my mouth shut as we move to the side of the dance floor. I've said too much already. But I'm torn. Turner's a good friend, so why should I let him think Kevin's typical, or even represents some kind of cutting-edge trend, when I don't believe it?

"He's unique," I muster.

"Well, there's unique, and there's unique," Turner says. "Rabbi Stu had a special reverse power. I don't think we knew what we had in him. He never took up much space in a room, and in crowds, he was almost invisible. But when we needed him, he was right there. It was as if he could see into your heart."

"That's what they said the great rebbes used to do— look straight into your heart," I say. "But he took his share of flak."

"And speaking of your more notable flak-throwers, look over there. She's throwing something tonight, but it's not flak."

Essie Sue is working the room with Kevin, clucking like a Mama hen.

I thank Turner again for rescuing me, and look at my watch. So far, this evening has lived up to all my dreaded expectations. I'm counting the minutes until we go home, but my misery isn't over yet. The one positive thought I've held on to tonight is the fact that I did drive my own car here—just to make sure this date deal isn't taken too seriously. I'm making sure I don't hang around for the cleanup detail—I figure Kevin will definitely get roped into schlepping flower arrangements into the trunk of Essie Sue's car, and I can be long gone before any complications arise.

Wrong. Essie Sue has anticipated this. She follows me as I'm getting into my car in the parking lot. She has Kevin in tow.

"I gave the rabbi a ride here tonight," she tells me.

"And since we're together," Kevin chimes in, "I'm sure you'll want to round out the evening with me. Can I get a ride home with you?"

Essie Sue gives me the "you promised" look.

"I'm really pretty tired," I try. "I think you can say we've had quite an extensive evening together already. And I'm sure you'll need Kevin's help in . . ."

"We understand," Essie Sue interrupts. "I don't need any help, and his apartment isn't out of your way at all so it won't take any extra energy to give him a lift."

I give up. "Sure, let's go," I say. "I'm only dropping you off, though."

Essie Sue gives Kevin a look. He winks back at her. Actually *winks*. I let my anger go to my foot and rev up the engine. He jumps in and she slams the door behind him so fast I could swear they've rehearsed it.

I'm kind of worried that he'll put his arm on the back of the seat or try to lean close to me, but he doesn't. I decide to be nice and make small talk, although there's nothing much I can say about the installation that won't have me either shuddering or giggling. I feel a little hysterical and on edge about the whole evening. It's exactly the kind of thing I'm very good at repressing, to tell the truth. Give me a week and I'll be telling myself it didn't happen. Probably with the help of some Doritos and sour cream dip.

I get to his apartment in no time flat—maybe I drove a little fast.

"Well, congratulations," I say, putting my hand out. "I guess you're officially installed." My mind won't quit picturing nuts and bolts.

"What did you think about my installation address?" he asks.

Somehow I'm not prepared for this, though I should have been ready with *something*. "Uh—it certainly had some startling elements." My curiosity gets the best of me re the Mary Baker Eddy routine. "Who called you in the middle of your speech?"

He beams. "I knew everyone would get excited about that. Actually, I called myself. There's a button you can press to test the loudness of the ring on your phone, and I just practiced pressing it while the phone was in the sleeve of my gown. I pulled it off perfectly. Even Essie Sue was surprised."

I'll bet she was. They say the medium is the message. What a medium we have in this man. And what a message. It makes you proud.

He's not moving, so as a hint, I push the button that unlocks all the doors.

"Bye, Kevin." I wave my hand cheerfully.

He's still not moving. Maybe I could walk around and open his door for him. Just as I'm getting ready to say good-bye again, he rotates in his seat and he's suddenly all over me. Mr. Finesse. He manages to plant a full kiss on my lips before I know what's happening. Oh yeah, and in the midst of all this, he takes his glasses off and puts them on the dashboard.

I think immediately of any number of physical things

I could do to him, but instead, I'm inspired. I grab the glasses and drop them directly under my foot.

"Kevin, if you don't get yourself out of this car in thirty seconds, I'm smashing your glasses."

"But they're Calvin Klein eyewear. They cost three hundred dollars."

"Out." I start counting.

"Give me my glasses."

"Reach down to get them and I won't vouch for your neck. I'll give them to you when you're out of the car and I have it locked. Then I'll roll down the window a couple of inches and you can take them."

Passion gives way to prudence. He gets out of the car and closes the door. I lock it and slip the glasses out to him.

"But it was a date. You owed me."

"Oh, I owe you all right." I start to shift out of Park. "And, Kevin. If you *ever* try anything like this again, you're toast."

I lean my head on the back of the seat for a minute to let my blood pressure go down, and off I go. It's midnight.

I don't even want to think about what's just happened. The funny thing is—I'm actually thinking the evening is finally over. If only.

chapter
32
....

I should be tired to the bone, but I'm not. It's like hitting your head against a wall and feeling *so* good when it's over. I'm luxuriating in my ratty old desk chair in front of the computer—all reminders of ballrooms and benedictions peeled off in the bedroom in exchange for my favorite pajamas. This particular soft cotton pair with the Betty Boop print is the mashed potatoes of comfort clothes—I only wear this when I'm particularly needy or particularly happy. I honestly don't know which I am right now. I just know that for a rare moment, my brain's in the here and now and not frantically jumping ahead or behind.

Nan announced earlier that she's staying awake for my full report on the festivities, no matter how tired she is or how tired I am, for that matter. She's demanding e-mail, and she doesn't demand very often. I'm very willing to comply—I'm just wondering how I can get it all down and manage to give her the—shall we say, full flavor of the evening.

I'm also expecting a fax. Nathan e-mailed me at ten o'clock tonight—probably while I was being a lil' old dancing fool in front of two hundred people. But we won't think of that—I'm preparing to have it all slip into oblivion as soon as I write Nan a complete account.

Nathan wrote me that he'd helped clean out Aunt Becky's closet and picked up some great old photos for his collection. He also found some more recent ones that Uncle Aaron took of Ida Sebran and her grown children on a Fourth of July picnic. Family gatherings were scarce in the summer—relatives were usually on vacation. Aaron and Becky always invited Ida when the rest of the family wouldn't be coming and they knew she'd accept.

Anyway, Nathan got the photos to satisfy my curiosity, even though they weren't anything he'd want for his collection. He says he's programming his fax to send the pictures at the cheap rates in the wee hours of the morning—he doesn't say when—just that I'll have them when I wake up tomorrow. He faxed me a photo of Ida's store last time, so now I'll have the whole schmear—people and place.

I'm thinking maybe the fax'll come through while I'm writing to Nan, when I realize that won't happen. My modem and fax are on one line, separate from my other phone line, so the fax will get a busy signal until I finish e-mailing on line and hang up—then it'll come through. Not that it makes a lot of difference—I'll have something to look forward to first thing in the morning.

I'm rating the events of the evening according to

Nan's tastes. The First Couple Dance will be high on her scale of must-tells, the Phone Call from the Heavens even higher, and Kevin's hitting on me a definite ten. I'm not sure where to start. I finally decide *not* to decide. I'll tell about the coronation just as it happened, and let the evening speak for itself.

I'm just describing the processional, when I hear a faint screech like a branch rubbing across a windowpane on a breezy night. Only it's not a breezy night. The sound is coming from the patio area in the back. I let it ride. Oy Vay's in the backyard, and she's probably scratching herself on something and making noise with her metal dog tag.

I'm continuing with the white spats and matching robe when I hear the shattering of glass. I freeze. I've been in perpetual clenched-jaw mode for weeks now, expecting the worst, but lately I'd almost begun to relax.

Oy Vay's not barking, which is no big surprise, since she's never met a stranger she didn't lick. Right now I hope she's cowering safely in the bushes, but I wouldn't bet on it. I feel drops dripping from my temples down my cheeks and under my pajama collar, even though the air conditioner's running full blast.

Any one of my neighbors would have a big old Texas-sized gun in hand by now. I'm a liberal. I think we can use knives, but I'm scared to go to the kitchen to find one.

My hands are shaking, and I notice they're still on the keyboard. Just to be on the safe side, I'm typing *"call police"* in the middle of my message to Nan, when the hairs on the back of my neck stand up. Someone is in the room with me.

I have two choices—I can either swivel around and see who it is or keep going. I click the Send icon.

I hear a very quiet voice.

"What's on the screen?"

"A work report," I barely whisper. I push the computer's Off button and the screen goes black.

The move takes only a second, but it has consequences—my visitor is not amused. Before I can turn around, two things happen. A rock-hard arm grips my neck from behind, and with the computer's modem now off, my fax starts churning out a page.

I'm being screamed at now. The voice is familiar, but I'm so stupid and panicked I can't place it. I twist enough to see a black turtleneck stretched halfway up the face and a black turned-around baseball cap on the head. I try to knock the phone off the hook, but it's being pulled out of its socket. The fax keeps churning— not that it'll do me much good.

The grip on my throat is tighter now, and I can't move my head. All I can see is the fax machine right in front of me. Chugging its way out of the fax is a large photo of three people standing in front of a table spread with food. Nathan has scrawled a large caption above the picture: "Ida and the Sebran Children—Fourth of July picnic."

Looking as serious as an American Gothic with pitchfork are, in order, a young blond woman I've never seen before, Ida Sebran with her gray hair in a bun, and Gus Stamish, Milt's head baker.

I now recognize Gus's voice, for whatever that's worth. He tears the page from its roller and screams at me again.

"My picture. Why do you have my picture?"

Even if I weren't being held in a death vise, I couldn't answer.

"You stupid, interfering bitch—just like your husband! Milt said you weren't coming around again—that it was over—no partnership. Then I get a call that you've gone across the country to spy on us—to our pathetic little white-bread, no-business bakery that's supposed to be my legacy. And now you have our picture? Where the hell did this come from?"

He crumples up the photo and I can feel him stuffing it in his pocket. For the first time since he grabbed me, I can see that he's not just nuts. If he's hiding the photo in his pocket, he's thinking pretty clearly. He must have a plan.

I figure if he hasn't choked me to death already, this won't be the way I'm gonna die. I try pushing his arm away far enough to whisper, "I can't breathe." He loosens his grip. I catch my breath and try to do something. Since I'm sitting, and he both towers over me and outweighs me by quite a bit, it looks as if my choices for doing something will only be cerebral. My most reliable kind, anyway, so it's just as well.

"Gus, can we talk about this?"

I don't think this is a great start. He's snorting like a bull above my head, with his arm still hanging, albeit looser, around my neck. Funny—I never thought he *looked* strong. I try again.

"What do you want from me?"

"No, what do you want from *me*?"

"The only reason I went to see your mother was because my cousins in New York thought I'd like to hear some stories about the old days. She's a friend of our family. My husband's family. When Milt . . ."

"Milt. Don't talk to me about Milton Aboud. Born Milton Sebran, my dear first cousin. Heir to my uncle's fortune—money 'Uncle' Irv took away from my father— his own brother. I changed my name and my life to make things right. What right did you have to pry into my life? Milt would have made me partner. He still can. With his money, I could sell all over the country."

Well, we won't talk about the fact that Milt only inherited the great sum of ten thousand dollars. The good news here is that nobody is mentioning the murders. Yet. If I can keep off that subject, maybe he'll feel he can let me go. At this point, I don't know he's been doing the killing. That's if you don't count my insides, my gut, my intuition, and my common sense. But I'm very good at denial, and I'm gonna pretend for all I'm worth. Not pretend—I really *don't* know yet. I have to keep telling myself that.

"Look, Gus, maybe we could . . ."

"Will you shut up? I'm trying to think."

"What if I signed over those partnership papers to you? Right now. I have them."

"Without Milt's signature? Am I a jerk?"

I don't answer that. More maniac than jerk, unfortunately.

"I'm getting us out of here. I hear too many noises out there."

"It's just my dog, and he's harmless." Oh, that was smart. So far he's outthinking me, signature included. Good work. I always wondered how I'd hold up under real pressure.

"We need to stay here and talk this out." I have no way of knowing if Nan got my message or not, but if she did, she'll ring here as soon as she reads it, and at least I'll know. Except that the phone's disconnected. It only took me five minutes to remember that. Very good thinking.

"Look, we've known each other for a while, Gus. I know I can help you."

"No one can help me. I've killed two people."

Uh-oh.

"I didn't hear it, Gus. I'm only interested in finding a solution with you."

I'm dead meat.

"I didn't want to kill the rabbi. It was his own fault. He was warned twice. He was a meddler, like you, so I had to keep him quiet."

And I hope you fry for it. So much for my former views on capital punishment.

"But why did you kill Marla?" I might as well know it all—it doesn't matter anymore.

"It wasn't supposed to be her, either. It was you, stupid. I had the bagel all ready for you, on top of your usual order. But you changed numbers with them after I'd already passed the bag to Milt."

Number 46—my age. Almond raisin. I remember. And it was a joke that I always ate the top one as soon as I got it. I can't say anything.

"I loaded it with almond flavoring to hide the taste. It would have tasted funny anyway, but by that time, it would have been too late. It was too late—for her. So she got it, and Milt was arrested for it the way he was supposed to be. I've found out I'm good at this."

He keeps going, cocky as ever.

"It was the lunch hour and all of us were filling orders, so it was easy for me to drop out of the line for a minute and head for the kitchen after I handed Milt your order. I wanted to be away from the counter when you got the bag."

He's not so cocky now, remembering.

"When I looked back and saw that woman step up in your place, I was still figuring Milt would set aside your bag for you. But I guess he mixed up the extras and gave her your bag instead of one of hers. If the idiot weren't so sloppy, you'd be dead now."

He's whining, yet. I change the subject—I don't need him concentrating on my death.

"If you hate Milt so much—"

"Why kill you two and not him? Because I would have inherited nothing. *Nothing!*" He's yelling again now. "I was his head guy. He leaned on me. He knew I was smart. Good with figures, too. He would have made me a partner, turned over the business to me before he went to prison. His wife had the kids to raise. Who else did he have? Until you came along."

His voice is rising.

"Get up!" He jerks me up and slides the steel arm down to my waist, holding me firm. Ugh—those arms are choking the life out of me. I remind myself never to be kidnapped by a man who's punched dough for twenty-five years.

"We're getting in my car. You're driving."

I've always been terrified of getting into a car with a bad guy. Looking at those Christmas-at-the-Mall stories on the news always made me think I'd do almost anything to avoid giving up all control and being forced into a car. I'd rather take my chances in the parking lot.

It's now or never. I'm staying in my own house, whatever happens.

As Gus starts to push me away from the desk, I jam my foot into the mass of spaghetti cables connecting my computer to my surge protector, my monitor, my printer, my modem, my phone, my speakers, and my label maker. I'm thankful I never put my own cables into efficient little cubbies.

Gus and I immediately fall to the floor and the lights go out. My lamp is connected to the surge protector, too.

I'm not in Gus's grip anymore, and I have the advantage in the dark. I know my own domain, or at least, I'm supposed to. He's grabbing for me. He does pile on me, finally, and he's smothering me with his weight. He's raised his head, and his hands are headed for my neck again.

I could say I planned the next thing, but I'd be lying. My arms are flailing, and purely by accident my hand curls around the leg of the dictionary stand. A thousand-page edition of the *Oxford English Dictionary* drops on his head. You'd think it would knock him out. He's down, but he's definitely not out, and his legs are on top of me.

I'm reenergized, though, because I hear sirens in the distance—Nan's come through for me. She's probably the only person on this earth I'd trust to convince the police halfway across the country to send help with sirens ringing. On the basis of an e-mail message yet. Who knows what she told them?

Now all I have to do is stay alive until they get here. Gus is trying to pull up and choke me again. I can't push him off me, so I'm stuck on the floor here. Before he puts his full weight on me, I need to act while I can still move. The only thing I see in front of me is a six-hundred-page WordPerfect 4.0 manual I've been using as a doorstop since 1985. What worked before could work again. I stretch out, and while he's trying to turn, I pull myself free. I aim the book at him and run, slamming the door behind me.

That should hold him for a couple of minutes. I'm headed across the street to use the phone, when I see a police car pulling up in my driveway. Next thing I know, I'm sobbing in Lieutenant Paul Lundy's arms while Oy Vay's jumping up to lick my face.

"I was on duty when the call came in," Paul says, "and a good thing, too. Your friend from Seattle said she was a lawyer and threatened to sue the whole department if we didn't listen to her."

I can't talk. At least, I can't talk until I remember there's a maniac semi locked up in my house. The most I can do is point toward the door and burble, "He's still in there."

chapter
33

....

E-mail from: Nan

To: Ruby

Subject: *Bad News and Good News*

The bad news is I haven't heard from you since I got that garbled call from you after the police left. If I had the money, I'd hop on a plane and come see for myself how you're doing. I called Lieutenant Lundy and he said you'll be fine, even though you're sporting a few really huge bruises on your arms and legs. He said not to disturb you for a day, and I've been sitting on my hands, but I'm gonna have to break down and call you anytime now if I don't hear from you. Write!

And when you do write, please clear up a few things for me, like how soon Gus's confession will clear Milt, what the deal was with Essie Sue clamming up, and how Marla got into all this. Not that I'm letting you off the hook—I'm sure my questions will go on ad infinitum!

Oh—the good news is I have a feeling I did okay on my LSAT—hope so!

Now, if I pass, all I have to do is apply to law school and beat the odds of one to twelve—that's how many they turn down for every student they accept—this seems insurmountable to me. If I don't make it, I'm not letting you forget you got me into this, you wretch. If I do get accepted, I have to figure out how to pay for it all. Maybe you can send me Care packages from the bakery. No almond flavors, please.

Seriously, I know this confession must have brought up lots of horrible memories for you, and that you're having all kinds of mixed feelings right now. I'm just thankful you're safe.

....

E-mail from: Ruby
To: Nan
Subject: *Passing the Bar and Baring the Past*

Why do you need to go to law school? I heard you told the police department you were already a lawyer and were suing the whole place. If that's any example of your persuasive powers, I'm not sure you need law school, babe. You can skip it all and go right to jury summation.

I just know you did fine on the LSAT. You'll get accepted, too—not to worry. We'll feed you until you graduate, and I'm sure you can get a loan for the tuition. What's a little lifetime debt?

Okay, I'll answer some of your questions, but honestly it's probably going to be ages before I can give you every detail of what happened last night. Bear with me. I'm totally wiped out, and you're right—I'm having a hard time dealing with all my conflicting emotions right now. I'm thrilled, of course, that Milt is free. We're planning a party at The Hot Bagel to celebrate our partnership, and of course, the fact that Gus is behind bars. I can feel safe again, and I'm thankful for that.

I'm having a harder time with other issues. It's not easy knowing for certain now that Stu was killed—I've had to mourn his death all over again—like opening a wound that had just started to heal over. And it seems so sense-less that Marla should have been killed merely because she took my place in the bagel line. I feel for her family—it must be hard to have closure when the whole process was such a random one.

You asked what the deal was with Essie Sue—I'm as-suming you mean why she seemed to hold back when the police wanted to know about Marla's past. Appar-ently, she was terrified of revealing some family secret concerning Marla's daughter Glenda. As I understand it, Glenda's father was not Marla's husband. Marla had married after she discovered she was carrying another man's child, and she never told Glenda who the real fa-ther was. Essie Sue had sworn never to tell Glenda, and after Marla was killed, she felt doubly responsible for keeping the secret. Plus the fact she really did believe Milt did it.

The fact that Gus was Ida Sebran's son has shocked Milt and his mother, as you can imagine. What seems weird to me is that Gus wouldn't have tried to take re-venge on Irv's three daughters instead of Milt. But the old male bloodline thing got him—he'd convinced himself that as Irv's son, Milt was the one who had what was rightfully his—the business and the money and that the daughters were secondary. Although who knows? He might have added them to his list after Milt. Gus claims his mother didn't know about any of this—he kept in touch with her by phone and told her he had a job here— that's all.

You saved my life, babe—even though they found Gus on the floor, still woozy from the WordPerfect manual, he could have come after me at any minute. This was not an easy man to keep down.

I'll write you more tomorrow—right now, I'm pulling down the blinds and diving into bed. Essie Sue and the rabbi just pulled up, and I'm not letting them talk their way in here.

Stay tuned.

Turn the page for a preview of

DON'T CRY FOR ME, HOT PASTRAMI

A Ruby, the Rabbi's Wife, Mystery

chapter
1
....

I know we're in trouble when the wooden handi-
capped ramp leading to the side entrance of the Temple
disappears—replaced by a swaying gang-plank. The sight
of Rabbi Kevin Kapstein hardly relieves my fears—he's
wearing a white yachting cap as he waves the board
members off the gang-plank and into a transformed
Blumberg Social Hall.

It only takes two *ahoy*s from Essie Sue Margolis,
Kevin's mentor and my worst nightmare, to convince me
I should be home watching *Law and Order* instead of
Kvetching and Chaos, as I've come to call our monthly
Board of Directors' meetings at Temple Rita. I gulp
down two aspirin tablets even before taking off my
jacket. This headache insurance hasn't worked yet, but
by now it's a habit.

"My Hearties, have I got a surprise for you!"

Ignoring the group shudder, Essie Sue, resplendent in
a crisp, navy blue sailor suit and hat, reaches for her third

metaphor of the night, and we've only been here five minutes.

"Now, Voyagers. I'm aware that you probably don't know what I'm talking about, nautically speaking. But you will."

"That's never stopped you before. Get on with the program."

Bubba Copeland has a short fuse and a long memory regarding Essie Sue and her fund-raising efforts. Essie Sue's still trying to commission a solid marble, six-hundred pound Queen Esther statue in memory of her late sister Marla, who dropped dead on the floor of The Hot Bagel a few years ago. We're all paying for it, in more ways than one. Her latest fiasco, a nationwide sale of reduced-calorie matzo balls, almost killed me last year. Literally.

"All will be revealed, Bubba, before we adjourn to the Social Hall for navy bean soup in honor of our newest fund-raiser."

"With Oreos?"

That's Mr. Chernoff—not that he'll sway Essie Sue one way or another.

"Stuff it, Herman. I'm talking originality here. The rabbi has already given his blessing to this event. You're going to love it."

I'm feeling queasy already. "So is this *event* going into the minutes as a done deal, or were we called here to vote on something? You're not planning to do an end run on the temple by-laws again, are you?"

"Please, Ruby—you and your constitutional concerns. Don't you have any imagination?"

"Yeah, I'm imagining that if this project has already

been blessed by you and Kevin, we don't have a chance."

"All right, then I'll do it by the book. Are you ready, Parliamentarian?"

About as ready as Rachel Gettleman will ever be, considering that her qualifications for the job were that her brother-in-law registered voters in Travis County from 1965 to 1973.

"Here's the surprise. I move that our new fund-raising project be a cruise of the Jewish Caribbean, featuring Saint Thomas in the U.S. Virgin Islands. Anchors Aweigh! Play the tape, Rabbi."

Before Kevin presses the button on *Naval Hymns from Down Under*, I press a point of order.

"Wait a minute—there *is* no Jewish Caribbean."

Essie Sue's ready for me.

"Of course there is. Jews sailed to the Caribbean before Poland ever knew a rabbi. I've researched this, Ruby. Don't think just because you're a rabbi's wife that you're the only Jewish historian around here."

"I'm no longer a rabbi's wife, and I don't know any Jewish historians in Eternal. Do you?"

My husband Stu was rabbi of the temple before he was killed a few years ago. It took all his energy to keep Essie Sue in check, but she's ruled the roost since Stu's successor, Kevin Kapstein, took over.

"Are you trying to say that Jews *lived* in the Caribbean, Essie Sue? That's a far cry from . . ."

"I'm not going to let you spoil my nautical evening, Ruby. There's a motion on the floor."

I can tell Bubba Copeland's catching my headache— the vein near his temple is enlarging as he speaks. "There's motion all right. I'm getting seasick. What's the deal here? Clue us in, Essie Sue, before I move to adjourn."

"I wanted everyone to catch the spirit first, but since you're all so oppositional tonight, I'll have to change my tactics. We need to go into Executive Session."

Rachel Gettleman doesn't look amused.

"We've never been in Executive Session before. Speaking as Parliamentarian, just what does Executive Session mean, exactly?"

"It means we meet without the rabbi."

"That's it? Am I supposed to escort him out?"

"I'll escort him out. Sorry, Rabbi. I was driven to this by extreme lack of cooperation."

"Point of order." Kevin's fighting back. "I want to lodge a formal protest. I rented this outfit."

"No way I'm dealing with a formal protest." Rachel's out of her seat. "Point of Parliamentary overload. What do I do now, Essie Sue?"

"Hold it, Rachel. Go check on the anchor carved in ice, Rabbi—this won't take long. My committee will reimburse you for the yachting suit."

"Your committee?"

Essie Sue manages to nudge Kevin out the door, squelch the last question from the assemblage, and ease Rachel back in her seat before staring down the room.

"Okay, people. This is serious."

"You're going to have a helluva time talking serious to a background of *Anchors Aweigh*."

"I know, Bubba, but that was merely window dressing to make the medicine go down. I'm not just fund-raising here. I'm trying to save the rabbi."

"Save him? From what?" Brother Copeland, younger

brother to Bubba—same substance, different style—pipes in where Bubba can't go. Essie Sue favors Brother over Bubba, so Brother can get more out of her.

"Gather round, everybody, and don't breathe a word of this. This is board business, okay?"

"Yeah, yeah. Just tell us."

"No, Bubba. I want sworn oaths from all of you. Raise your hands."

Curiosity overcomes common sense, and we all dutifully raise our hands to swear confidentiality. Right.

"Do you all swear not to tell, not ever to tell what I'm going to tell you, so help you God?"

This is too much. "I'm not swearing to God on this, Essie Sue."

"Okay, Ruby, so we'll swear on my copy of the *Jewish Daily Forward*—it has a national circulation. Good enough for you?"

I refrain from raising my hand altogether, but she ignores me and pulls out a huge file folder from her briefcase at the end of the table.

"People, these are the top-secret results of a questionnaire I submitted to a temple focus group at my own expense. I made copies for everyone. Read it and weep."

"Focus group? Who do you think you are, Dick Morris?" Bubba's reaching for his copy as he speaks, of course.

"This is the way things are done in the modern world, Bubba. We're nothing if not *with it* here at Temple Rita. I regret to inform you that my survey shows our beloved rabbi's job approval rating has fallen to an all-time low."

"What did you expect?" Brother yells. "He squeaked

by the Rabbinic Selection Committee by a majority of one."

"He did not. He was voted in unanimously."

"Oh, sure, after you made the secretary erase the vote and put in *Unanimous* on pain of death."

"That was a courtesy. All organizations do it. This poll was scientifically calculated to compute the Rabbi's charisma quotient. On the first question, 'Is our rabbi as dynamic as you thought he would be?' Rabbi Kapstein unfortunately scored one percent."

"This is too painful, Essie Sue. Just let us read it to ourselves."

"No pain, no gain, Ruby, but if you insist, I'll give on that point."

I don't think it can get worse, but then I read the sample questions:

Leadership Ability—If Rabbi Kapstein were to the temple as Moshe Dayan was to the Israelis, would you follow him into battle? Yes: 2%.

Intellectual Prowess—Do the Rabbi's sermons pique your curiosity? Not really: 97%.

Does the Rabbi stimulate our mission as a light unto the nations? Dim: 98%.

"Pardon my asking, but just who in the congregation did you focus on for these answers, Essie Sue?"

"They shall remain nameless, Ruby. End of story."

"So what are we supposed to do with this?"

"That's why we're here. The rabbi is obviously not putting his best foot forward."

"I'd say he was putting his foot *in* it."

"Be that as it may, Brother, the man needs help, and I, for one, feel he's misunderstood. That's why this cruise is going to be his salvation. He'll be our trip guide, show-casing his leadership abilities, and he'll educate us in the history and culture of the Jews of the Caribbean—that takes care of the the intellect thing."

Essie Sue flicks a red-manicured little finger at the Par-liamentarian, who reacts in Pavlovian fashion:

"There's a motion on the floor. All in favor, say *aye*."

No hands go up.

"Does anyone here want to go through the rabbinical selection process twice in three years?"

All hands are up, including, I have to say, mine.

Essie Sue, beaming, goes to the door.

"Ahoy, Rabbi—bring on the navy bean soup."

chapter
2
....

E-mail from: Ruby
To: Nan
Subject: Cruisin' for a bruisin'

Congrats on snagging that plum of a second year legal internship—even though it's my personal opinion you don't need it after working for a lawyer all those years. I guess the real benefit will be in drafting material on your own, yes? And in maybe becoming indispensable to the firm for the future. I hope they give you the independence you want.

Don't bite my head off, but now that you're in the groove, school-wise, shouldn't you be making room for a personal life? I haven't heard the word *date* in your vo-cabulary since you gave me your recipe for granola mix. Look around in class—you never can tell who might be lying in wait.

Update on Essie Sue's cruise plans: things are more relaxed in that arena since she accepted my terms for assistance—that I help make the arrangements as a non-traveling participant. I can keep my cool as long as I know I don't have to *be* one of her little tourists. I've done some internet research on the cruises, but so far, she hasn't taken any of my suggestions. She must have an angle. I'm waiting for the shoe to drop.

....

E-mail from: Nan
To: Ruby
Subject: Et Tu?

Pardon me, but shouldn't *you* be making room for a personal life? Unless you count Kevin as a *date* and not just a nut—and I assume you'd rather be dead than do that—your own granola pile looks a little sparse to me, babe. Answer. (And we're not counting your three-legged golden retriever here—Oy Vey's cute, but this is not the companion I see in your future.)

As for my not needing this legal internship, surely you're not equating my former employer, Stanford P. Jerk, Esquire, with my *experience*, are you? As a role model for malpractice, maybe. I'm trying to forget everything Berke taught me.

Anything new from oceanside?

....

E-mail from: Ruby
To: Nan
Subject: Funny you should ask

This just came in the mail, on a blue paper flyer:

MASS MAILING TO MY CRUISE COMMITTEE FROM YOUR CHAIRWOMAN

Yo Sea-mates!

I've just learned through the kosher grapevine that my long-lost cousin, Harry Goldberg, now known as Captain Horatio Goldberg, is one of the few (who knows? maybe the only Jew) to be captain of a bona fide cruise ship. Captain Goldberg is following in the footsteps of Christopher Columbus, who, as you know, was probably also Jewish.

Captain Goldberg is currently sailing the Caribbean for BARGAIN CRUISE LINES—We Pass Waters Where Others Fear to Tread.

The best news is that after tough negotiations behind the scenes, the cruise line is willing to go wholesale for fund-raising purposes, and we have sealed a discount deal.

This is confidential. More later.

Essie Sue Margolis.

So, Nan, what do you think the odds are that she had this deal with the cousin up her sleeve all along?

Ho Ho Ho!

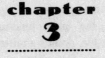
*The Hot Bagel is the closest thing to a community cen-*ter we have in our little town of Eternal, Texas (fast becoming a suburb of Austin since the freeway was expanded). I hang out here a lot since I became part-owner of the place with my friend Milt Aboud. In the non-bagel half of my life, I'm a computer consultant, which used to be a unique job in Eternal until half of Silicon Valley moved here to work for Dell Computer. As long as I pay attention to both my occupations, I can get by—unless your definition of *getting by* includes a personal life.

Essie Sue's attempts to make me relive my entire adulthood as a clergy wife by becoming the Bride of Frankenstein (excuse me, make that bride of Kapstein) continue to fail abysmally, but that doesn't stop her from trying, despite the fact that I'm not the least bit interested in Kevin. If he'd stop trying to do Essie Sue's bidding, he'd know he feels the same way about me. From time to time, he deigns to look down favorably upon me from the heights of his ego, but then realizes I have a mind inside my head, not a mirror. Kevin's idea of compatibility with a woman is not the usual *I likka you, you likka me*—with him, it's more *I love me, you love me, so we'll both get along famously.*

Tonight we're being not-so-subtly matched again, at Pastrami Piracy, the latest fund-raising extravaganza where, for twenty-five dollars a raffle ticket, anyone with two feet and cash can sign up to win ten whole pastramis as second prizes, or the first prize of a Caribbean cruise straight from Bargain Cruise Lines. I told Essie Sue her attempt to combine the word *piracy* with one of her notoriously rigged raffles would be a tad too realistic, but here we are.

My business partner, Milt, didn't speak to me for three days when I said yes to this event, but I figured it would be good for business. So far, we've sold a lot of bagels to the hundred people who've showed up, but Milt doesn't care.

"I'd rather starve than work with that woman."

"Just think—she'll be away on the cruise and you won't have to see her in here." Pretty pathetic, but it's all I can think of as a comeback.

He ignores that. "She even went to San Antonio to order those pastramis, instead of getting them through me—can you believe it?"

"You should be glad, Milt. If anything went wrong with them, she'd blame you."

"You've got a point. She told me she thought of raffling pastramis because they went with bagels, but when I pressed her, she admitted she got a deal on ten of them from some connection through Mexico, so she worked them into the *concept*."

"Oh, great. She should have put 'win at your own risk' on the raffle tickets."

"I just want this evening over, Ruby. Whoa—I'm outta here. She's coming this way."

Milt disappears into the kitchen and I'm stuck, as usual.

"It's a fabulous evening, Ruby—even having it here." Essie Sue's glowing.

"Gee, thanks, I think."

"We've sold a bunch of raffle tickets, not including the ones we unloaded before the event. We might have done even better if I'd had time to decorate the bakery like a cruise ship."

"You already did that at the board meeting. Besides, I had a hard enough time getting Milt to have the party here—there was no way he'd agree to let you come in and tear the place apart."

"He's a boor. Thank goodness my niece Glenda didn't marry him." Milt and Essie Sue go way back, but that's another story.

"Can you get a stool for me, Ruby? I'm going to stand on one of the tables."

"Excuse me?"

"I want everyone to see me when I draw the winning tickets."

"Sit on the table, Essie Sue—they can still see you."

"Nightclub singer style? Okay. It might look good with this slit skirt, if I position my legs right. At least I've still got my figure."

That's a dig at me, even though there aren't as many

pounds between us as there are years. It's just that those pounds are all around my waistline in one bunch. In return, I get to eat like a normal person and she gets to call a lettuce leaf lunch. I decided a long time ago it was a fair tradeoff.

She swivels herself up onto a table in the center of the room and crosses her legs. The shock value of the nightclub routine seems to have passed the crowd right by, but she forges ahead anyway.

"Ladies and gentlemen, welcome to Pastrami Piracy. We're giving away ten whole pastramis and one free chance for piracy on the high seas, where Blackbeard robbed and plundered. These hot pastramis will feed seventy-five people if you slice them thin enough—and you should, if you don't want a coronary."

I don't know about anyone else here, but I'm thinking this is not such a great come-on for future cruise-goers. She's supposedly planning to make money from commissions on the discount cruise tickets she sells—and raffling the free trip should whet people's appetites—if the pastramis don't get there first.

"And now for the main event." Essie Sue has even uncrossed her legs for the big announcement. "The owners of Bargain Cruise Lines have graciously donated a lovely stateroom as First Prize in our raffle. And to those of you who don't win, I can only say that for a few measly dollars—money you'd undoubtedly squander on dull necessities—you can go along with our lucky winner and sail in the footsteps of the pirates."

Wow, she always did have a way with words—that last should really reel 'em in.

"To conduct the drawing of the winning ticket, I'd like

to introduce a distinguished surprise guest." She jumps down from her perch on the table and plunges into the crowd, emerging with a balding, bespectacled little man who's having difficulty holding onto her hand. In fact, he's being dragged at a rapid pace. Essie Sue doesn't fool around.

"People, this is History Professor Willie Bob Gonzales, of Buda Community College in Buda, Texas, our official lecturer for the cruise. Professor Gonzales's specialty is the *Jews of the Inquisition and What Happened to Them.*"

The professor looks a little uncomfortable at having his life's work summarized so brilliantly, but he's apparently already discovered like the rest of us that it's safer to go along. He's not invited to say anything, but Essie Sue still has his hand so he can't leave.

"As you know, people, the Caribbean is full of Spanish Jews, and this is all going to be very intellectual. The ship also has two casinos." I guess this was thrown in for the benefit of the rest of us—Essie Sue is not dumb when it comes to soliciting funds—but it does appear to have thrown Professor Gonzales. He tries to shake loose, but she's stronger than he is.

"My cousins, the Bitman twins of Buda, have known Willie Bob Gonzales for several years during his tenure at the community college, and they recommend him highly. Just to make sure, they'll be sailing with us—right, Professor?"

The Bitman twins undoubtedly carry the same genes as their cousin—at least enough to make Willie Bob go pale at the mention of their names. He nods and tries for a smile at the crowd.

"So that's already myself and my husband Hal, Professor Gonzales, my twin cousins, our spiritual leader—Rabbi Kapstein, and the winner of our raffle, who will be on our way to the high seas. I'm sure the rest of you will be joining our ranks soon. I certainly expect all the pastrami winners to fork up fares for the voyage—it's only fair."

With that sort of encouragement, you'd think this crowd would be heading for the exits, but they're all gathered around, tickets in hand, for the big drawing.

Professor Gonzales sticks his hand ten times into the empty five-gallon ice cream carton Essie Sue has decorated as a rum barrel. Ten lucky winners come up to receive certificates for their pastramis. I know it's only coincidence that all of them are either related to Essie Sue or are members of the fund-raising committee. Not that she rewards her own—before the lucky winners can reach their hands out for the certificates, they're required to sign up for the Temple Rita Cruise. The actual pastramis will come whenever the shipment can get through Customs, I presume. If the recipients are lucky, maybe the pastramis'll be delivered while they're away in the Caribbean—then they won't have to eat them.

"And now for the piece de resistance. I shall ask Professor Gonzales to step down, and call forward our own Rabbi Kevin Kapstein to draw the Grand Prize Winner."

Kevin, in a black pin-striped suit, vest, and power red tie, formally shakes Essie Sue's hand, waves to the crowd, and with an obviously well-rehearsed gesture, plunges his hand into the ice cream carton and hands the winning ticket unseen to Essie Sue.

I should have seen it coming when Kevin had a big

smirk on his face before she even looked at the paper.

Essie Sue holds the ticket aloft. "The winner is—our late-lamented-rabbi's wife, Ruby Rothman. Ruby, come on down!"

SUS ___ ERT